PRAISE FOR *PEACE LIKE A RIVER*

"At the center of this excellent novel is a long-withheld secret that both strains and binds two generations of fathers and sons. Scott Gould tells his story with wisdom, empathy, and artistry. He never condescends to his characters; they are fully human in their complexities and hopes. Deeply moving and memorable, *Peace Like a River* is an outstanding novel."

—Ron Rash, bestselling author of *Serena* and *The Caretaker*

"*Peace Like a River*, Scott Gould's captivating novel, explores father/son dynamics from every angle, and like the river so beautifully described, delivers memorable surprises at every bend including a long kept childhood secret. Memorable characters, lively humor, and a cat named Wille Nelson; what's not to love?"

—Jill McCorkle, bestselling author of *Old Crimes* and *Hieroglyphics*

"*Peace Like a River* is a deftly written, immersive story of a man navigating the treacherous waters of intimacy as both a son and a father, burdened by the past while finding footing in the present. With the raw elegance of a Lowcountry ballad, Gould's distinctive prose sings of mistakes, regrets, and making peace with it all. I found myself lingering over lines threaded with poignancy, hope, and humor. This is a novel to savor."

—Kelly Mustian, bestselling author of *The River Knows Your Name* and *The Girls in the Stilt House*

"…a poignant and, in this day and age of father-knows-nothing, timely rallying cry for the uncompromising importance of being a dad and what that means in terms of navigating death, aging, guilt, and loss while at the same time summoning up the guts to be hopeful despite it all."

—*Southern Literary Review*

"Fans of father/son classics like *Independence Day* and *A River Runs Through It* will be pleased to find traces of those works (yes, both a river and a road trip figure prominently), but *Peace Like a River* carves its own path, delivered with a distinct Southern accent and a fearless willingness to wear its heart on its sleeve. This is one of those rare books where you feel like you know everyone personally and want, somehow, for everyone to win. I was rooting hard for all of them."

—Keith Lee Morris, author of *Travelers Rest* and *The Dart League King*

"A soulful, funny, earnest quest for connection, Scott Gould's *Peace Like a River* answers old wounds with new growth as three generations of Southerners find common ground on South Carolina's Black River."

—Stephen Hundley, author of *Bomb Island* and *The Aliens Will Come to Georgia First*

Also by Scott Gould

Strangers to Temptation
Whereabouts
Things That Crash, Things That Fly
The Hammerhead Chronicles
Idiot Men

Peace Like a River

Scott Gould

Regal House Publishing

Published by
Regal House Publishing, LLC
Raleigh, NC 27605

ISBN -13 (paperback): 9781646036066
ISBN -13 (epub): 9781646036073
Library of Congress Control Number: 2024944581

Cover images and design by © studiochi.art
Author photograph by Escobar Photography

Printed in the United States of America

Regal House Publishing, LLC
https://regalhousepublishing.com

To June Maryann Wilson, Sofia Lane Wilson,
and Bennett James Wilson

"Thousands have lived without love,
not one without water."

—from "First Things First" by W.H. Auden

Part I

The Old Man

1

Thom is reading headlights again. It's this thing he does, and at first, it's all clever and cute, but after a solid hour of him reciting makes and models, you consider pitching him through the open window. But no matter how strong the desire to toss annoying thirteen-year-old boys from a moving pickup, you can't. He's your son. There are laws against that sort of thing.

For a reason no one has figured out, Thom can predict what kind of car approaches at night, with only a quick glance at the headlights in the distance. And he's never wrong. Oh, he might be off by a year or so, but he's always spot on with the model. He did not inherit this particular, peculiar gift from me. I never like to guess what's heading in my direction.

It probably surfaced in his mother's end of the gene pool, so I'll blame her. I also blame her for that h. When she showed up at The Cotton Bottom on fake karaoke night and told me she was pregnant with a boy, she threw out a follow-up question: "You have any thoughts on a name?" I didn't say a thing because I couldn't form words after receiving that kind of news. A couple of days later, I called her and said Tom is a fine name for a boy. I liked the sound of it—quick and sudden, like half a clap. I had no idea she would take my suggestion, and I didn't know she was going to add that h and throw the word off balance. Now, his name sits there like a lisp on the page. She said, "You get three letters, I get one. Stop complaining."

So I did. I never had much of a leg to stand on with her.

We're driving a dark, smooth stretch of Sumter Highway just beyond the Dabbs Crossroad, the arrow-straight part. You can see a couple of miles in either direction. I almost died on this road in high school. My buddy had a '68 Camaro convertible that could top ninety in half a heartbeat. One night we were out, going too fast, and this deer leaped out of the dark and into the headlights just as my buddy punched it into fourth gear. The top was down. Deer parts ended up splattered everywhere. It's a wonder the deer is the only thing that died.

"That's #6, Elwin," Thom says. I didn't realize I was talking out loud about the Camaro and the deer. That's another annoying thing Thom does—he numbers my stories. He says he gives them all numbers because he gets tired of me repeating them. He calls me out. He does weird things like that—numbering stories, reading headlights.

"It's a good story," I say.

"It's still #6, Elwin. It will always be #6," he says. He calls me Elwin. I guess *Dad* is too much to hope for when you see someone every third weekend and a couple of weeks in the summer.

"Dodge Ram," Thom says. "2012, I believe. The headlights are elevated slightly, so I'm assuming a lift kit is in play."

Sometimes you look around and wonder how the hell you arrive at a certain place. Me, sitting in a faded Chevy pickup with no air conditioning, a couple hundred thousand rough miles on the original engine, beside a surprise son I had way too late in my life with a woman way too young for me, a kid who constantly scribbles in a teeny notepad with a gnawed-on golf pencil, who shoves those white buds in his ears most of the time, the ones wired into his iPhone, listening to whatever it is strange, smart thirteen-year-old boys listen to these days.

I'm only being honest. Thom is strange and thirteen. And smart. Not that those qualities are normally stitched together. Or maybe they are. Maybe I don't have a clue what normal looks like at thirteen. When I was that age, I had a best friend with a fake eyeball who jumped off a bridge twice, and the second time, he disappeared under the surface of Black River and never rose again. That's strange, too, but it's another story. What I mean to say is, strange, shitty things happen at thirteen, and some of them never work their way back to the light.

Thom's right on the money, I think. A jacked-up Dodge

Ram roars out of the darkness, eating up its lane and a sliver of mine. "My mistake, 2013," he says.

His mother is named Roma (after the city, not the tomato, at least that's what she told me), and we never talk that much, but when we do, she says things like, "You know your son is on the spectrum," and I say things back, like, "Aren't we all, Roma, aren't we all," and that's where the conversation usually ends. If Thom is on a spectrum, then it's a place all his own, and he's the lord and ruler. I'll say this for him, he seems pretty goddamn happy on his spectrum. Give him his earbuds and a golf pencil and that kid smiles like a cat burglar about to make a clean getaway.

The Lowcountry darkness throws off a dank, heavy smell, especially this time of the year, when a blanket of humidity settles like a moist, bad mood over the road and the swamp and the ragged soybean fields that line the asphalt. It smells of sour mud and greasy water and all of nature's mistakes that percolate in the floodplain just off the river. To me, it smells like home. Not to Thom.

"Jesus, Elwin," he says, plucking the buds from his ears, "that's rude." I have no idea what he is talking about, a relatively common occurrence between the two of us. "You passed flatus."

"It's just swamp funk," I say. "We're almost there."

"You must mean swamp *gas*. Methane and hydrogen sulfide and CO2," Thom says, showing off from his reserved seat on the spectrum. (Another relatively common occurrence.) "And please," he says, drawing out the word *pleeeeeeease* into a thin whine, "don't tell me again how when you were a child, you could smell the paper mill all the way from some village called Georgetown. The stinky paper mill story is #12." He sticks his earbuds back, then scribbles in his little notebook. That's how Thom begins and ends most conversations—with his earbuds. Sometimes I want to crush those bastards under my shoe like a couple of expensive white cockroaches. But I would never do that. I *think* about it, but I would never do it. That's become a habit of mine the older I get: thinking about things I'll never do. And I can't lie, it gives me some comfort.

Every third weekend I pick Thom up at Roma's house on a Friday afternoon after I finish at the store. (Go ahead, laugh. I'm used to it. I'm an old English major working in the shoe department in Dillard's, but I got tired of teaching and decided selling shoes was as humanitarian a task as explaining Homer to bored teenagers. Plus, it's only part-time, and I set my own hours.) On those Fridays, Thom waits on the front stoop, his little suitcase tucked between his knees, looking like a kid who's been sentenced to a stretch of hard labor.

And every third weekend, we go through the same routine. I believe it breaks the ice that tends to form between visits. I'll say, "Need help with your suitcase?" and he'll say, "It's a valise, Elwin," and I'll say, "What kind of kid uses the word *valise*?" and he'll say, "One who knows how to pack properly, Elwin." Then he'll screw in his earbuds and smile. His grin is crooked on the left side like mine.

I also get Thom for two weeks in the summer, the weeks on either side of the Fourth of July. Roma calls it her Independence Celebration. The two of us never got married. She says, "Hey, we got along fine for one night. Why ruin a perfect record?" But it's really because of the ages. She'd be an idiot to marry somebody twenty-five years older, and she's no idiot. I mean, I'm not feeble and broken down yet, but sometimes I sense assisted living snapping at my heels. Roma would never call me old. She's not mean-spirited. But I possess working mirrors in my duplex. I look more like Thom's granddaddy than his father. None of us can help that fact. How do we get to these places? Sometimes you have to ask yourself that.

"Honda Accord," Thom says. "Brand new."

We are nearly at the turnoff toward Mouzon. He's right. An Accord zips past us, bright and shining in the dark. It's too quiet in the truck, so I start talking, which is another thing I do—fill up quiet spaces with words. Mouzon was where Radley tried to kill us in his Camaro convertible forty-something years ago.

It's a story worth re-telling. I'll fill up some empty air. Good stories are still good stories, even if your own son tags them with numbers or blocks them out with his earbuds.

I may look like Thom's granddaddy, but I'm not. He's got one of those, and that's why we are on the road. The Old Man is dying, allegedly, and I haven't smelled this swamp in fifteen years. The last time I was on this highway, I was heading the other direction, for good, I thought. Thom has never met his grandfather, my father. We are both driving into new territory.

"A Dodge Charger, one of the newer ones, Elwin. Could be a cop," Thom says, pulling out a single bud. He points through the windshield with his pencil. I let off the gas, even though I'm nowhere near the speed limit.

Sure enough, twenty seconds later, a Charger. The kid rarely makes mistakes. He doesn't get that from me.

2

I'm not a big fan of Linda McCrea, and she knows it, so I was surprised to get a call from her a couple of days ago, out of the blue. At the time, I wondered how she'd found my number. When I was a kid, Linda was the widowed neighbor a couple doors down from the house I grew up in. After my mother died, Linda McCrea became something else. She started seeing The Old Man—or he started seeing her. They saw each other. Doesn't matter. That road always runs in both directions, no matter who's at the wheel.

They never moved in together or got married. According to my long-lost brother, Eli, who was still living at home at the time, they sort of wandered between each other's places like restless ghosts trying to decide which house to haunt. I was the only one bothered by the fact that they set up their odd housekeeping while my mom's sweaters still hung in her closet. The first and only time I talked to the Old Man about it, he said, "Don't bunch your panties up, Nancy." Translation—don't worry about shit that isn't your business. Now that I think about it, that was the last time I had a conversation with him.

When Linda called, all she said was, "You best come on down. Your daddy is pretty sick."

I said, "How sick is pretty sick?" and Linda McCrea couldn't answer because she was trying to choke down her crying. I didn't recall Linda being a crier, even when her husband passed away. I heard the sob snag high in her throat. She said, "If you want to say a proper goodbye or anything, you..." and never finished the sentence before she hung up. I know it took a lot for her to call, and that crack in her voice told me something. She was upset, and she wanted me to feel the same way, but that wasn't going to happen over the phone.

The Old Man never had great timing. The call came a day

before the official commencement of Roma's annual Independence Celebration. When I got in touch with her and explained what was going on, Roma said, "Do I have to go over this again? I'm a single mother—a completely single mother—and I need a break," and "I have plans. I paid big deposits I can't get back."

I said, "What do you want me to do?" I thought it was a decent enough question. "My father could be dying. I have to go down there."

"Thom says you don't even like your father," she said. Roma has a way of getting to the point, no matter how sharp it is.

I launched into the whole bit about how the Old Man was hard to take growing up—all of his coming and going, his disappearing and reappearing—and how I didn't really hate him, just never understood how he could act the way he did with my mom and me and my brother, and swear to god, I thought she was about to tell me which number *that* particular story was, but all she said was, "So take Thom with you. Period, end of story."

"I'm not sure the best time to meet your granddaddy is when he's about to die," I said.

"That might be the absolute best time," Roma said.

Women who barrel right to the point and bad timing and sick fathers and unexpected, teary phone calls. They pile up and conspire against you, and you end up burning your vacation days on the road with Earbud Son, who doodles swamp-gas notes in his tiny little pad with a golf pencil he chews to a nub.

Thom breaks the silence inside the truck. "Where will we be staying, Elwin?" he asks, looking up from his notebook. "I'm not sure I'm comfortable staying in a stranger's house. That feels a bit reckless." Thom isn't comfortable with a whole lot of things. He got all bent out of shape packing for this trip, because I couldn't tell him how long we'd be gone. He stuffed that valise of his but had to add a bigger bag. That threw him off. It probably bothered him that his mother's Independence Celebration luggage was already stacked and lurking in the hallway. Maybe the sight of her suitcases next to his made him suspect the two of them were parting ways for good.

Kingstree doesn't have much in the way of accommodations, which should tell you something. Not a place people visit all that much, much less spend the night. Kingstree is a pass-through town—folks on the way to the beach or the interstate, stopping only for the barbecue at Brown's or to put their boat in at Gilland Park. The people who stay overnight are deer hunters or corn seed salesmen or nostalgically confused Yankees, or at least that's the way it used to be. Online, one place was described as a "boutique" hotel, but the pictures they posted didn't scream boutique to me. The only other option was a motel, the old Kingstree Inn.

I tell Thom we are going to stay at the Kingstree Inn because back when I was a kid, I had a paper route, and I used to fill up the machine in front of the motel with copies of the *Charleston Evening Post.* I'd eat a glazed doughnut and drink a Coke at the counter before I pedaled for home. "#10…again," is the only thing Thom says, and yeah, I know he's heard it before, but a little respect for the past would be a welcome gift every once in a while.

From the looks of it, the Kingstree Inn has been crumbling for years. The columns fronting the entrance are shedding their paint in feather-sized strips, and one lists so far to the right, it can't be holding anything up. I remember the building as being red brick, but the exterior appears to be wrapped in vinyl now, some of the long aluminum panels pulling away from the walls. Somebody must have bought the Kingstree Inn and put it on cheap life support, like a patient in a lengthy coma.

The lobby of the motel is no improvement. The furniture is too big for the space, and every piece is faded and covered with stains that suggest bad intentions and body fluids. The wallpaper has been painted over ghostly designs escaping from behind the dingy colors. The eye-watering odors of cleaning solutions and something skunky fill the air, but frankly, it's a welcome change from the funk of the swamp we just drove through. I've forgotten how many smells this town has.

The man slumped at the front desk is about half my age,

skinny and white and wearing a T-shirt with a homemade tie-dye job and a ponytail pulled so tight, his forehead might split. He looks like a fellow who spends most of his life fighting weariness—his eyes doughy and half-closed—and when he raises his head to greet us, the effort makes him wince. I wonder when he last slept.

"Reservation?" he says, the question weighted down by hope and desperation, like if I say yes, Thom and I could win a prize.

"Nossir," I say, tossing a little respect his way—hoping Thom will notice, but like usual, his earbuds shut him away from the world of words. "Just hoping you have a room for a few days. Not sure how long exactly."

The fact that we plan to stay more than a single night sends a jolt of financial adrenaline through the desk clerk, and he jumps to his feet. I notice the name tag on his T-shirt. He is *Marvin*. I wouldn't have expected him to be a Marvin, but I try not to have preconceptions about people. That's gotten me in trouble before. And there's a little girl hunkered behind the counter on a bright orange beanbag chair. She's an airy, bird-like creature, and the beanbag is on the verge of swallowing her up. She wears cheap, dollar-store sandals, probably a size four and a half, I'd say. (I know feet and their sizes at a distance.) Her nose is planted in a book that's thick as a brick, and she doesn't look up from the page she's on. If I had to guess, I'd say she was twelve or thirteen years old, but I could be wrong. Her size might tell lies about her age. I catch Thom peering over the counter at her. His eyes seem to be working better than his ears.

"How many rooms, please, for you and your…?" He pauses for me to fill in the blank.

"Just one. He's my son."

Marvin nods at Thom, which spurs Thom to pull the buds from his ear.

"I'm sorry, excuse me?" Thom says.

"I was telling him we need one room, because you are my son," I say, and Thom looks put out that he has to share a room with me. I want to remind him that first, I'm not made of money, and second, he was a plus-one on this trip. Another couple of things I could blame his mother for.

The way Marvin glances from me to Thom and back to me again—doing his motel industry mental calculus about our ages and our appearance—I'm sure he believes I'm engaging in human trafficking. But god bless him, Marvin values his cash register more than his suspicions, because he takes my credit card, maybe a little too fast. I'm waiting for Thom to embarrass me, yell out, "FOR THE LOVE OF GOD, HELP ME! I'M HIS PRISONER." But all he does is sigh loud enough for us to hear, including the little girl being eaten by a beanbag chair, and she looks up for the first time. She sights over the top of her glasses, and I think, *She already needs reading glasses. She must be wearing her eyes out.*

She notices Thom too. I can tell by the way she instantly sticks her nose back inside her book when she catches sight of us. She moves quickly, like a person who's been caught doing something wrong. When I glance behind the counter at her, I see that she's reading *Great Expectations.* I like her immediately. If I'd ever had a classroom full of her kind, I wouldn't be at Dillard's, handling people's feet.

"One room, and what did you say…four nights?" Marvin asks, and I tell him that sounds good, although it could be shorter, depending on how it goes with the Old Man and his *pretty sick* sickness. Could be longer too. I have no idea what I'm doing here or how long I'll be doing it.

Thom pipes up—I knew it was coming—and says to nobody in particular, to the air, "What is her name?" He points in the direction of the beanbag chair with his golf pencil. Marvin doesn't say a word, instead nods toward the little girl, who looks up from her *Great Expectations.*

I swear Thom's standing on his tiptoes, trying to look taller. Beanbag Girl doesn't say a word. Instead, she snorts. At least, that's what it sounds like, a cross between a laugh and sneeze. Then she tosses her cropped-off dark hair and dives back into her book.

I'll say this for my son. He doesn't throw in the towel. He says, "I'm a huge fan of that boy in the book, Pip. That Pip sure has staying power," and re-screws the earbud into this head. I feel a wave of fatherly pride rise in my chest when he gets in the last word.

3

The only new feature at the Kingstree Inn is its name. Now the place is called The All Excellent Inn, and I wonder if Marvin is a man comfortable with irony. There is nothing *excellent* about the place. It sounds more like a poker strategy than the name of a motel. Our room, number 113, faces the railroad tracks, and I wonder how often we'll hear the train blow by in the night. "I'll bet the 4:15 still comes by on the way to Georgetown," I say, and I expect Thom to give me the number for that story. I'm positive I've told it a few times.

Instead, he pulls the buds from his ears and says, "This room resembles a crime scene, and I refuse to sleep here." My son is right. Nothing good would ever happen in this room. Stains seem to be a theme at The All Excellent Inn—the carpet, the tops of the furniture, the tub and toilet are covered. It smells like something is rotten in a place we can't see.

"Don't pull back the bedspread," I tell him. "I brought sleeping bags. We'll sleep on top of whatever's hiding under there."

I don't have to check my watch to know it's too late to head to the hospital. When I called Linda McCrea to tell her we were coming, she said the Old Man was in a private room and the hospital had very strict visiting hours. "But," she said, "he might be leaving soon." As I was about to tell her that sounded like good news, that maybe it was a sign of improvement, she said, "He wants to die at the river."

I didn't recall Linda being so direct all those years ago. To me, she was just the woman who carpetbagged her way into the house where I grew up, where my mother took her last breath. I remember her as being flighty and out to lunch most of the time, but maybe she grew a new voice with the Old Man, a new spine.

"I won't sleep a wink here," Thom says, "therefore, I'll sleep in the truck. You must realize in some part of your brain that this isn't healthy for me on a number of levels, Elwin." He drags his valise and suitcase toward the door.

"It's too hot and mosquitoes will eat you alive with the windows down," I tell him. "What would your mother say if I let you sleep in the truck?"

"Where have you brought us, Elwin? Pests, smells, bloodstains in the tub, rude little girls, people on the verge of dying? This is hellish, Elwin."

I don't know why he always calls me Elwin. Okay, that's a lie. Roma explained it to me in that way she has of reporting news that strangles your ego. She said, "It's simple, Elwin. You don't see him enough to be a father. Once a month, two weeks in the summer? You are, at best, a genetic acquaintance. You should be glad he calls you anything. Be happy with the little things, Elwin." When Roma explains the world, I feel like a first grader. And I've got a quarter century on her. I've seen things.

"I know you don't want to be here, and don't take this the wrong way, but I didn't want to bring you. I'm not sure seeing your grandfather this way is smart. In fact, if you don't want to see him, that's fine. We can just tell your mom that you said hello to him and be done with it." Thom's eyes widen slightly at the thought of lying to his mother. "Okay, maybe we won't do that. But we have to make the best of this. I'm not real pleased about being here either."

"It's life, Elwin. Doing things that are distasteful is part of the cycle. I will lie on the side of the bed farthest from the door. When the drug-addled thieves break in, I want them attacking you first," he says, then hoists his suitcase onto the bed and pops the latches. I admit, I've never looked in his little valise when he comes to my house on the weekends. It always felt like a violation. But this? I can't turn away. The kid has folded his changes of clothes and put them into big ziplock freezer bags. When he starts pulling the bags out, I see he's labeled them with a Sharpie. Some have the days of the week printed on the plastic. Others are labeled *Extra Underwear* and *Washcloths* and

Swim Trunks. There are some smaller sandwich bags too. One of them is labeled *Misc*, and I spot extra shoelaces and a couple of fresh golf pencils.

"It's rude to stare, Elwin," Thom says.

When I look at Thom and see the things he does—packing in ziplock bags and carrying spare shoelaces because lord knows, we've all been in situations where we say, *I wish I had an extra shoelace*—I wonder if he's really my son. There isn't an organized bone beneath my skin. I don't wonder about the days ahead, when I might need to replace a broken shoelace. Do other people look at their kids and say, *Who the hell is this person and where did he come from?* Sure, his mother and I did get along fairly well that one night, the night she said she liked older men because they had settled into the world, but I never figured that thirteen or so years later, I'd wind up in a motel room with a son who labels his baggie of underwear.

As if he's reading my mind, Thom says, "It's called organization, Elwin. I feel better when some parts of my future are planned out. You've brought me to this hell, Elwin. At least I know what I'm going to wear as we plod through it."

I guess everybody searches for comfort where they can, even thirteen-year-old boys.

"Whatever works," I say. I don't open my little duffel bag. I don't want my son to see the kind of mess his father can make.

4

Thom repeats that there's no way he's going to be able to sleep. Five minutes later, he's snoring and trying to swallow his tongue—another thing I never notice when he stays at my house—these gagging noises he makes, like a grizzled old man. Sleep is too far away for me to grab. Too much buzzes behind my eyes to close them.

I hear the night unfold outside The All Excellent Inn: a couple of slamming car doors, a howling dog and a second dog answering the first, a cat bothering one of the dogs. A single siren whines its way north, out of town. I have this thing for directions, for knowing the points on a compass. There's a value in knowing where you are. Maybe that's as weird as packing in ziplock bags. The air conditioning unit hums beneath the window, and a train finally rumbles through, long after midnight. We are close enough to the tracks to feel the floor vibrate slightly, like a mini-earthquake. I'm surprised it doesn't wake Thom. I used to hear that train every night when I was a kid. During the day, when the trains came by, Lonnie Tisdale and I threw dirt clods through the open windows of the caboose when it slowed to a crawl. This was a couple of summers before he drowned. Thom calls that story #8.

A security light shines behind the shade Thom pulled down as tight as it would go. "Someone could still see around the edges," he said, with a hint of panic in his voice. Just as I'm about to close my eyes and make a serious attempt at getting some sleep—when the dogs stop howling and the siren disappears and the train tracks quit vibrating—I hear a small, slight shuffling outside the door of room 113, and everything on my body slams to a halt, including my lungs.

I hold my breath and glance at Thom. He's still chewing his tongue. In the glow of the window, a silhouette of somebody or something stops in the narrow frame of light. I think, *Maybe if I rush the door, I'll scare it away*, but I don't believe I can move. The silhouette shifts slightly, and it suddenly strikes me, *It's the little girl from the beanbag chair*. I recognize the tiny outline she casts. If I imagine hard, I think I can see her glasses glint in the dark when she tries to peer through the slit in the curtain. Thom was right. You can see around the edges.

Then something slides under the door. I make an instant list of the bad things it could be. Spiders in an envelope that will find their way to freedom and bite us in the middle of the night. Or anthrax. Maybe a ransom note: *If you want to leave room 113 alive*. But it's delivered by a little girl who reads Dickens in a beanbag chair. I'm silly to be afraid of something so small.

She walks away—I hear her plastic sandals flapping the rough sidewalk—and it takes me half a minute to breathe normally. My eyes are used to the dark, so I walk to the door without having to click on a light. I should put on shoes; the moist carpet sticks to my feet, and I don't want to think about the fluids responsible for that. I rest my ear on the door and hear nothing but the air conditioner humming through the wood.

On the floor just inside our door is a small sheet of paper. No spiders that I can tell. I pick it up and can't make out the words, so I lean toward the window and open the slit a little. Light from the parking lot blooms onto the page. No ransom note. It's the title page torn from the little beanbag girl's paperback copy of *Great Expectations*. At the top she's written something. Perfect little handwriting.

This book belongs to Lily Salters

I think, *Well, that's an interesting way to introduce yourself*, and I wonder if I should tell Thom that little dark-haired girls are sneaking around and sliding notes under his door? I'll wait. That's just good parenting, I tell myself, putting off confusing things until the light of day. I fall dead asleep in seconds, as if the shadowy appearance of Lily Salters has calmed me down.

5

Linda McCrea is convinced I'm not supposed to like her. Linda McCrea assumes a lot. She has that look on her face when Thom and I meet her in the lobby of the hospital the next morning, that expression that says, *You have good reason to be mad at me.* The look a dog has when he greets you a couple seconds before you find the garbage all over the kitchen floor. Guilt and resignation, braided together. But I don't know why. I haven't seen Linda McCrea in years and years.

I was not born in this hospital. They tore down Kelly Memorial a long time ago. This is the replacement, on the southeast edge of town, modern and shiny. The lobby gives off that new-hospital smell, fresh carpet and paint with a tinge of hope mixed in.

"Oh my," Linda says, "how long has it been?"

I could tell her exactly: fourteen years, sixty-seven days. I did the calendar math before Thom and I hit the road. Fourteen years, sixty-seven days since my mother's funeral. I remember Linda sitting alone in the pew behind the family like a sentry, keeping watch on our backs. It wasn't much of a family lineup—just me and the Old Man and my brother Eli and my mother's sister who drove in from Memphis. The day after the funeral, my aunt filled a huge cardboard box with Spanish moss and carried it back to Tennessee. I like to imagine a tree somewhere in Memphis draped with gray moss from my mother's front yard. I should visit her, if she's still alive.

Six months or so after the funeral, Linda and the Old Man started wearing a path between their houses. This was the house on Logan Street, with the little hill in front. I remember Eli calling me and saying, "Nobody is making a big deal. He won't even talk about it. Maybe he's just sad or lonely." Eli's voice hummed low and hoarse, so he wouldn't be heard by the Old

Man, or maybe by the ghosts in the house. I said, "Little quick to try and get happy." The phone went dead for a few seconds until Eli said, "You need to come see it for real." But I never did. I'd made my final exit the week after my mother's funeral.

"And who is this?" Linda says, her voice racing up a musical scale to a note that could crack glass. I don't remember Linda McCrea being this energetic. She's too old to have a voice that high. The shrill pitch works its way into Thom's earbuds, and he snatches one of them out.

"This is my son," I say. "Thom."

Thom cocks his head at Linda as if he's examining a rare bird that just landed at his feet. I see the folded-up piece of paper still in his hand, the torn page from Lily Salters's *Great Expectations*. Thom hasn't let go of it since I told him how it ended up in room 113.

"I'm here to meet my grandfather," he says, then replaces the earbud. I've tried to talk to him about being a little more personable when he meets new folks, especially adults. Most times he doesn't say a word, so this is an improvement.

"Can he hear me?" Linda asks.

"No," I tell her. "That's how he keeps things under control. He listens to music, blocks things out. Roma says he's on a spectrum. I'm not so sure." Beats me why I'm giving Linda McCrea so much information so soon.

"Roma?" Linda asks, and I can tell the name throws her. That happens to most people. They think tomatoes instead of a woman. "Anyway, he best hurry if he wants to meet your daddy. We're not sure which direction this thing is heading, but it ain't a good one."

"What room is he in?" I say and take a step toward the elevators.

"Well," Linda says, "that's a whole 'nother story."

I'm not sure which rule book for conversations Linda follows. She seems to be waiting for me to say something, while I'm waiting for the rest of my Old Man's *'nother* story.

Thom pulls one bud from his ear. "He's not here, is he,"

he says and it's not a question. He stares right at Linda, which ignites her discomfort. She wiggles where she stands and looks to be considering breaking into a run.

"How'd he know that?" Linda asks, taking a step backward.

"He's not here?" I say, a little louder than I'd planned. Thom shoots me a look that suggests he's proud of me for raising my voice. I'm thinking we should start over—Thom and I should walk into the hospital lobby and say hello to Linda and thank her for taking care of things until we got there; then and only then, ask her which room the Old Man lies in. We've gotten off track.

Linda says, "Your father got antsy. You know how he is. Well, you remember how he is, I mean. Anyway, he decided he had no intention of staying in this place. He got all pushy for somebody to take him to the river, and he knew I wouldn't do it, without, you know, something official from a doctor, so I went down to the cafeteria to get an egg sandwich. Did you know they weigh the sandwich, then charge you by the ounce? I make very light egg sandwiches because I don't put any mayo on them, just a dash of tabasco. Mayo is one of your heavier condiments. Anyway, when I come back, the room was empty, and I'm guessing he got in the elevator and caught him a cab to the river. He lives down there, you know. He doesn't have any friends to speak of. Anyway, I ate my sandwich, and now, here we are. I didn't think I should go hungry just because he wants to die at his river house."

Thom has never been around people like this, ones who tell rambling stories in large, looping circles, people who will tell you everything except the one thing you need to know. I would think he'd be frustrated, but Thom has a wide grin spread across his face, the widest I've seen in years. He's completely fascinated with Linda McCrea.

"So we don't really know where he is? I mean, he could be anywhere. He may not have gone to the river," I say. "Wait, he has a house there?"

Before she can answer, Thom says, "Which bread weighs

more, wheat or white?" And the way Linda looks at him, I can tell she has found a kindred spirit who magically arrived from a 'nother world.

6

Everybody insists at once.

Linda insists that she drive us to the river house, that she won't hear of us taking two cars in the same direction. "That ain't nothing but a waste of good gas," she says.

And Thom insists on sitting in the front seat of her ancient Mercury Cougar. He can't take his eyes off Linda, and the fact his earbuds stay screwed in his ears while he stares keeps Linda off balance. I take a place in the big back seat, where the Cougar smells like memories of its past. I pick up bitter magnolia perfume and BO and—hand to god—fish, like someone's been cleaning their catch on the upholstery. There are even hints of barbecue sauce and beer. I smell my father beneath it all, which makes me reach for the button to lower the window.

"You run it down too far, it won't come up again," Linda says over her shoulder, then she reminds me it's probably been years and years since I've laid eyes on the Old Man's little spit of land at the riverbank.

"Do you live at the river now too?" I ask. I'm so far behind on things. My brain works in a weird way. I tend to forget how long it's truly been. I've come to believe that Kingstree—and the people and my old house and the river—exist in suspended animation, waiting for me to make my triumphant return. Maybe this is the true definition of nostalgia, the silly delusion that nothing changes, despite how many pages of the calendar are torn away. "What happened to the old house on Logan Street?" I say.

"Young couple knocked on the door one Sunday evening and told your father, 'If you ever think of selling your house, we'd be interested in looking at it.' They gave him a little card with their name and phone number on it. The next week, he cut a deal with them. A really good deal."

"He made money?" The Old Man never made money from his deals in the past.

"Did he sell it by weight?" Thom says, and Linda gets a kick out of that. She giggles so hard, she almost loses her breath. The two of them—they already have something going on, and I'm not included.

Linda angles off the highway, and the road turns to gritty sand and grows bumpier, a washboard vibration I feel through the seat, all the way into my teeth. The Mercury squeaks on its ancient springs. Outside my half-open window, thick trees—hardwoods and pines—pinch in on the road, narrow it down. The Mercury barely has enough room to squeeze through. Thom hits the button on his window

"There's no problem with that one. You can let it go all the way," she says, almost sounding proud of Thom. Damp air clouds into the Mercury, air so soggy and thick I could squeeze it between my finger and thumb. We round a bend in the road (perhaps a little speedier than I would have liked—the back end of the Mercury chuttering slightly into the curve), and I see a small building perched on stilts, an odd, faded spider shape. The last time I was here, there was nothing but a plank-sided shack with a rotting foundation and dirty glass in half the windows.

Things have changed. So much for nostalgia.

7

At first, all we spot of the Old Man are his skinny bare legs stretched out on a rickety end table. Then we round the corner of the deck and get the full view of him in his hospital gown, a frayed Texaco trucker hat pulled low over his eyes, his feet covered with hospital-issue slippers, probably mediums. He still has a beard, but it's trimmed now, instead of how I last saw it, hanging wild from his face, and now it's gone completely white. We can't see his eyes behind the aviator sunglasses, which are trained down the slope, toward the river.

"Ain't dead yet," he says without turning to us. He takes a sip from the Old Milwaukee in his hand. "But I'm in serious negotiations with it."

He doesn't pull his gaze off the water, which I guess means we're all supposed to look that direction. Like a trio of mechanized dolls, we turn toward the river. I haven't thought much about what my father might say to me after fifteen years, which means I haven't given much consideration to what I'd say back. I suppose I should treat this moment better, give it its due. But I keep my mouth shut, and suddenly I'm a kid again, standing around and watching and waiting on my father. Some things *don't* change, no matter how many days evaporate into years.

"River's down," he says. "Cypress trunk." This is instantly familiar, him throwing out information in a mysterious code few can decipher. When I was Thom's age, I spent a lot of time trying to put together the puzzle pieces of the Old Man's words.

"Ah, the rings. I see what you mean," Thom says and steps around me on the narrow porch, pointing toward the far bank.

That gets the Old Man's attention. "Well, look at you. Better late than not the hell at all," he says and drops his glasses down his nose, his eyes on Thom. The eyes don't look like they belong to an old man sentenced to die. They're the same as I remember, clear and focused on things no one else sees, usually something in the distant future. The rest of him is a wreck. Now that we are closer, I see his legs are thin-skinned and blotched, and his chest sinks into itself. Whispy-white tufts of hair poke from beneath the greasy Texaco hat. Something is eating away at him from the inside, and it's about to work its way out.

"I'm Thom, and you're my grandfather that everybody calls the Old Man, and I'd say you are very much alive, though there are rumors to the contrary," my son says, one earbud dangling at his chest, the other planted in his ear. He's giving the Old Man half his attention, which for Thom is a generous chunk.

"I used to paddle across the river with an axe and tie up to that big cypress there and chop a stripe every time there was a new high-water mark. That's how I kept up with things. The one way up there is from 2015. The river came through the front door that fall. Linda was beside herself," he says, and she chuckles from behind me.

"I'll get chairs for everybody," she says and disappears into the house.

I would never have recognized the place. The last time I saw it was right after my mother's funeral. And years before then, the first time the Old Man showed me this piece of property, it was a secret he'd squeezed for years. That was after a funeral too. Lonnie Tisdale's. I don't know what it is about this parcel of land and funerals. There was no building the first time I was here, only a cement slab with a ratty tarp strung over it. He told me if I ever needed a place to come think, I was standing on it. He told me this was where he escaped to work things out, and sometimes working things out took weeks. He confessed to me that this was where he came all those times he disappeared from our house. He put me in the black water that day like an odd baptism. Told me to stay where he could see me, to not get out of sight. He included me in his secret club.

A couple of years after that, he built a shack twenty-five yards off the sand bank, where the wall of cypress trees kept the swamp at bay. He did all the work, scrounging roofing tin and lumber from broken-down tobacco barns he'd come across when he drove around the county. He called it a fishing shack, but I never once saw him with a pole in his hand.

But now, this. A little house on stilts another fifty yards farther from the shoreline to protect from high water—except in 2015, I guess. Curtains frame the windows. The Old Man has curtains? A porch with a table to prop his bone-white legs on. Linda comes in and out of the door, and I catch a whiff of the interior of the house. It smells like a hundred good meals.

"It's Thom with an h," Thom says. "You should know that. It seems to make a difference to people." He cuts his eyes at me.

"Consonants are cheap to come by," the Old Man says. "How old are you now? I haven't been kept up to date real good." It's his turn to shoot a look at me. I am caught in strange family crossfire, tracers zipping at me from the generational bushes.

"Thirteen," Thom tells him.

"You sound advanced for thirteen," the Old Man says.

Thom sits in the chair Linda slides beside his grandfather. "There are a number of theories regarding that very fact. Some say I exist on a spectrum. You might hear the word *precocious* tossed about now and again. I'm not quite sure what I am, and I'm certainly not sure *where* I am."

"Well, Thom with an h, we're all where we're at. Ain't another place we can be," the Old Man says. "Pleased to meet you."

"Likewise," Thom says. They both settle into their chairs and stare at the water like they've known each other for decades.

This is not what I had in mind for their first meeting. I imagined something a touch more cinematic. I thought there might be a moment when they studied each other for resemblances. I thought there might be an awkward hug. Or, in Thom's case, there might be his usual weirdness that would have to evaporate before he actually spoke to the Old Man. Hell, at the very least, I thought I would do the introductions. But this is what I get. Like I said, it doesn't pay to predict. They act like aging college roommates who don't need to catch up with each other—they just need to sit for a spell and study the water.

The Old Man hasn't said a word to me yet, and I don't know if that's a good omen. I say, "You're looking good, Pops," and he says back, "If you were a better liar, we'd all appreciate it," so we shut up and watch the cola-colored river flow by in the quiet.

8

Thom doesn't care about breaking up the silence. "What do you want me to call you?" he says. "What is killing you?"

The first question, I suppose every grandchild deals with at some time or the other, but not at thirteen. I can't see Thom going with any of that *PawPaw* or *Grandpappy*. I don't think he even knows the Old Man's first name. He's never asked me.

Thom should have tiptoed around the second question. Linda makes a fluttering sound with her mouth, as if a bird is trapped and flapping behind her teeth. "Thom!" I say, with a little edge to it.

"What?" he says back, completely unaware that you don't normally ask the details of someone's demise.

"It's fine," the Old Man says and pats Thom on the knee. "I don't much care what you call me. I'll answer to just about anything. My mother called me bubs. Both of my kids called me the old man when they thought I wasn't listening. Linda calls me old bastard and sweetie, depending on what time of the day it is." Another flutter escapes from Linda's mouth.

Each time she makes that noise, Thom does a quick, quiet clap in his lap. He loves Linda. He's probably going to want to take her home, like a pet he found.

"The doctor has a whole file about what's wrong with me. He says I got numbers that get too high when they supposed to go low. Others go low when they supposed to rise. I can bottom-line it for you, son. All those things under my skin that been clocking in regular for work for eighty years are about to go on strike, and there ain't a thing nobody can do about it. Quitting time at the factory," he says, tipping the Old Milwaukee can to his mouth.

From behind me, Linda says, "You're not supposed to be drinking. Doctor told you that."

"What's that, honey bunch? Would I like another one? You read my mind, darling," he says, shaking his can over his head. Linda grabs his empty and disappears into the house, mumbling under her breath.

"I would prefer to call you Private," Thom says, doing his usual thing—connecting dots no one else has even spotted yet. He realizes he's confused us and sighs that he has to waste time with an explanation. "Elwin has a wobbly desk in his house and inside a drawer in said desk is a stack of photos. One of them shows you in your Vietnam conflict days, a private's stripe clearly visible on your shoulder. Well, my assumption is the photo is of you. Yes, Elwin, I was snooping. There is not much else to do on the weekends at your house."

The Old Man likes it. He smiles and salutes, "Whatever you say, sir," but he never takes his eyes off the river. I always wished I could know what he sees in that water, but like when I was a kid, there's nothing but trees and a river the color of old coffee, and it doesn't seem to be moving, that is until some flotsam from the world—a leaf or a plastic soda bottle—creeps by on the current. Something that slow and quiet always scared me back then.

"Your daddy take you on the river yet?" the newly christened Private says.

"I have never been on a river, period," Thom says. "But it's not Elwin's fault. My mother doesn't like to do things that require her to range far from home. And she doesn't like Elwin to do them either."

"You need to get this boy on the water. He'd probably take to it like..." and Private pauses, searching for a comparison.

"Like Moses," Thom says. "Truth be told, I do not know the Bible well. I have read through it once, and if I recall, there seems to be an abundance of water imagery, usually cataclysmic in nature. Floods and the parting of seas that come back together to drown armies, or whales that swallow men in the ocean. The Moses story caught my eye. Water was helpful in that case. An escape route. You're familiar with Moses?" Thom asks the Old Man.

"He needed a better boat," Private says and pulls at the tab on the fresh beer Linda puts in his hand. The Old Man's synopsis of the Moses story seems to satisfy them both. I should be happy they are getting along so well.

"Listen, you can't just check yourself out of the hospital," I say. "You need to be back where a doctor can watch you."

"I didn't check out. I left," he says.

"Well, you need to be where the doctor can keep an eye on you."

The Old Man tilts his beer. He leans away from the river and peers over the tops of his aviators at me. "Son, are you listening to yourself? You keep saying the doctor needs to watch me. I'm paying good money for people to *watch* me. That's about the stupidest thing I've ever heard. Just watching, that's all they do. Oh, and waiting. Waiting until they don't have to watch anymore. Well, I took all the pressure off everybody. They don't need to watch, and they don't need to wait. I can do all of that on my own."

"For how long?" Thom says, and again, the Linda mouth-flutter erupts from behind us.

"Jesus, Thom," I say, "can you just keep your mouth shut for once?"

The Old Man ignores me. "I've been thinking about that," he says. "Tell you what, Thom. You keep an eye on the countdown." He puts his beer down on the arm of the chair. Linda shuffles behind him and slides a coaster underneath it. He unstraps his wristwatch and hands it to my son. It's an old-school Timex. "You got to wind it once a day. Don't let it run down. You tell me when the time is right."

"For fuck's sake," I hear myself saying aloud. Linda is so uncomfortable, she begins pacing on the small deck, mumbling.

We both see it. The Old Man and Thom are on the same page, which is odd for two people who didn't know each other ten minutes ago.

"It's almost noon," Thom says, spinning the band on his tiny wrist.

"See, you're a natural," the Old Man tells him, and it doesn't much matter what I say at this point. I don't think anyone would listen.

9

It starts coming back to me. How the Old Man talks in mazes that lead to dead ends and unexpected turns. How he never says what you want him to say, what you expect him to say, like *Well, damn, it's been a long time. It's good to see you again* or *That boy of yours looks a lot like you* or *Maybe I should go back to the hospital.* The Old Man never gives you what you want, or even what you need. You have to find that on your own.

But—and I count this as a good thing—Thom seems happy. They both do. *Well, of course, they are,* I think. *The two of them are the kind of people who are happy on the fringes of the world where there's plenty of room to maneuver…*

I've resigned myself to the fact that Thom is never going to hang around people who do normal things. His mother tried that until she gave up. Thom will wear your ass down, I'll say that for him. The kid is a grinder. I think he may have gotten that from me. I tend to put my head down and move forward no matter what pushes back. Roma told me one time I was a redneck Sisyphus. She didn't think I'd get the allusion because I sell shoes, but she was wrong. She didn't know about my moldy English degree. Sure, I push a lot of rocks up a lot of hills, but I hope I'm smarter than Sisyphus. I know when to quit. Sometimes the rock just gets too goddamn heavy.

We are taking the Old Man back to the hospital, that's for certain. He doesn't seem like he's camped out on death's door, but what do I know about that sort of thing? I should be more somber about the whole impending death situation, more respectful. I mean, Linda summoned me home because he was (supposedly) on his last legs. And those particular legs don't look like they'll last long. He was always skinny, with his Vietnam-era stomach problems and eating only soft foods for the last fifty or sixty years, but those legs. It's a wonder they hold him up.

"We should probably head back," I say to no one in particular.

"Well, of course you should," the Old Man says. "That's what you're good at—making tracks." There he goes. Cracking open a door, hoping I'll walk across the threshold and stumble face-first into an argument.

"We can talk later. It's been a long time," I say. He'll want to know what's kept me away, and I could use an answer or two in that area myself.

"Don't wait too long," he says, swirling the Old Milwaukee in his can, his eyes on the river. "Time is short, right, Thom?" Thom looks at the watch hanging heavily on his left wrist, like it's going to perform some sort of trick.

"I could make some lunch," Linda says. "I'm sure there's something in the fridge."

"Nothing but leftover mashed potatoes and gravy from Colonel Sanders and half a jello mold," the Old Man tells us, effectively shutting down dinner plans. "Nobody's hungry anyway, sweet cheeks."

I nod at Thom to get out of his chair when I suddenly remember that my truck is in the hospital parking lot. We are at the mercy of the Cougar. "Linda, can you run us back into town?"

"Hold on," the Old Man says. "Thom, you ever seen a Black River boat? There's one tied to the dock down there. You go take a look. Give me a quarter hour or so with your father. Put a timer on me."

I'm surprised Thom wants to walk down to the dock alone. He rises from his chair and checks his new watch again. He looks to me for permission. Another surprise. A little raise of his eyebrows and a breath of hesitation, one earbud still in, the other dangling on his chest. I see Lily Salters's title page crumpled in the same hand that holds his phone, but I don't see his notebook. Must be in one of the big pockets on his shorts.

"Fine with me," I say. "Be careful."

"Don't worry about me, Elwin," he says, then walks down the gentle slope to the dock that extends thirty feet into the current. The last time I was here, there was no dock, just a narrow sand beach at the end of the hill. Linda has disappeared into the house. She didn't make a sound when she left, no flutters from behind her teeth.

"Your son calls you Elwin," the Old Man says. "What we supposed to make of that?"

Another of the Old Man's cannonballs screaming over my bow. "You probably shouldn't talk about what you don't know," I say. What I want to tell him is, *You ought to be real familiar with sons who do unusual things*, but it's probably bad luck to throw darts at a dying man.

"He's an interesting kid. I suspect there's a lot banging around in his head. But he's not all that strange. At least, not as much as Roma led me to believe," and he stops to take a sip. I wasn't expecting that. He isn't just firing warning shots now. He's torpedoing me head-on. "Yeah, that's right. I talk to her, every six months or so. She called *me* first. Looked me up and got in touch. Can you imagine that? A woman I've never met calls me out of the blue and gives me updates on a grandson I ain't ever met. She said at the very least I was due a heads-up." He raises slightly to get a better look at Thom down at the dock. It's more of a pier than a dock—no rails or steps, just a wide walkway extending like a tongue over the dark water.

"CHECK OUT THE BOAT IF YOU WANT!" the Old Man hollers, then coughs quietly into his fist when he tries to suck in a breath. Thom waves at us.

"I'm not sure that's a good idea," I say. I don't even know if my son can swim. Why do I not know if my son can swim?

The Old Man pulls off his glasses again. "You given much thought as to why you're here?" he says, staring straight at me. "Let me answer that for you. You're here because you want to be standing in the room when I pass, standing there so you can say, *I'm here and you're gone and that means I win.* Am I right? Think you're winning something?"

I take a seat beside the Old Man. I can tell he had to summon up some energy for that last shot. Now that I'm closer, I see how tired his eyes are.

"I came because Linda called me," I tell him. "I'm here because I thought I might be of use, somehow. I didn't come to watch you die."

"Your momma died. You left. Eli left. Everybody leaves," he says, not much above a whisper.

"We don't have to rehash all that," I say, trying to let us all off the hook, at least for the time being.

"That's part of your problem. You never want to rehash anything. I remember that about you. Any time you made a mess, you looked for the nearest rug to sweep it under," he says. "Or at least that's what you did until you ran off. Well, you got a kid now. Can't run from that. You'll see."

He turns his attention back to the river. "Shit," he says, rising quicker than I thought possible on those creaky legs and craning his neck downstream. "Shit damn." He wet-coughs again into his hand.

At the dock, where the boat floated seconds before, the space is empty, the water splitting quietly around pylons. Between the dock and the first downstream bend, the river is empty, and fear rises from my stomach into my throat. Not even a ripple on the surface, no sign that there was ever a boy or boat on the dark water.

10

I*'ve killed my son.* That's my first thought. My second is, *the Old Man killed him. It was his boat and his rotten cleat.* My third thought is, *Roma is going to kill me.*

Each of these thoughts spins in my head when I run down the slope to the dock, as if sprinting to the site of Thom's disappearance will help. Maybe I think that I can look downstream and see him and yell something useful—how to avoid strainers in the current or how to check for cottonmouths before you grab a limb. Or how to swim.

I trot up and down the length of the dock, like a nervous dog working up the courage to leap in the black water. There's no sign of Thom. In a way, that's good. I can assume he's still in the boat. He may not know how to swim, but floating in a boat doesn't take a lot of skill. The river takes a sharp right turn fifty yards downstream. "HOW CLOSE IS THE NEXT HOUSE?" I scream up the hill toward the Old Man. He stands at the deck rail, his hospital gown billowing sail-like in a sudden breeze.

That's because he never panics. When I was a kid, he warned me about panic and how it killed more people in Vietnam than anything else. More than once he said, "Boy, remember this… you panic in the jungle and you turn into a punji kabob real quick."

He hollers back that there is a place six or eight bends downstream, and I remember that's how people on the river measure their distances—by the number of bends.

Panic is making me forget things, like how I left my phone in the Mercury, so I haul ass back up the hill, past the porch, and snatch my phone from the front seat of the car. I punch in Thom's number, and the call goes straight to voicemail. The Old Man is back in his chair, stroking his beard. My son who has never been on a river, probably never been in a boat, is floating down Black River, and my father sits down and sips his beer.

"You asked me about houses," he says, "but you didn't ask about nothing else. There's a hunting shack not too far downstream, where the river narrows down. He'll pull out there. Bet you twenty dollars."

I can't stop moving. "Linda can drive me to the hunting shack," I say, taking a couple of steps toward the Cougar.

"Linda doesn't hunt," he says, and that's when I feel something erupt in my chest. I start yelling at my father.

"MY SON IS ON THE RIVER AND YOU HAVEN'T GODDAMN MOVED!"

I can't see his eyes behind his dark aviators. "We can get you to the shack. It'll take about twenty minutes because we have to go out to the blacktop and double back. Quicker in the jon boat I got under the house. Paddle down. It's all dinged up and got a real slow leak, but you'll be fine. Long as you don't panic. I'll get Linda to drive us to the shack. You need to drag that boat down the hill. There's a paddle in it and a soup can to bail, if you need it. I'd help you," he says, "but remember, I'm dying and everything."

I'm already down the steps, dodging the stilts under the house, looking for the jon boat. When I drag it down the hill, the Old Man calls out, "He'll be fine. Stop worrying. He's a kid in a boat on a river. He's right where he should be." He starts to tell me how the hunting shack should be empty this time of year and how it isn't hard to spot, but I'm out of earshot when I hit the dock. I want to yell at him that Thom isn't like other thirteen-year-old boys, that he never acts like you expect him to, but it would be a waste of the breath I need for more important things.

I remember this boat. The Old Man has owned it forever. Decades ago, he bought it from a guy in our neighborhood for next to nothing after a tree fell across it. The Old Man banged out the dents in the aluminum and straightened it as best he could, leaving it with a slight warp that makes it hard to paddle. All of the rivets are crusty and rusted, and I watch water burble through a few of them when I slide the boat into the water. I don't check under the seats for black widows, so I pray I don't feel anything crawling up my leg. I almost tip when I first climb in because I'm moving too fast—I'm panicking—but in a couple of strokes I find a decent balance point and lever all my weight behind each pull on the paddle. The boat's so warped, if you want to go straight you aim a little to the right. The current begins to help. In Black River, the current always fools people. On the surface, the river looks slow and lazy, but just beneath where you can see, it tugs toward the coast with a steady desperate energy.

Every few paddle strokes, I stop and dial Thom's number. Straight to voicemail each time. I give up on that and begin calling out his name, which violates the quiet of the river. The sound echoes off the walls of thick-trunked cypress trees flanking the riverbanks, bouncing back to me in a way that sounds almost mocking. I scan the banks for a sign that Thom is out of the boat. I don't know what I'll do if I find it turned over and pinned against a cypress knee, but I can't think about that. There aren't any sand beaches yet, just thick swamp and stagnant bog with barely any separation from the actual river channel.

I finally spot a ribbon of sand when I round a bend, but no indication that Thom beached his boat. Would he even know how to do that? Maybe I don't give him enough credit. He solves most problems he bumps up against, but in a runaway boat on a strange river—that's a lot for a kid like Thom to figure out. *A kid like Thom.* Why can't I just say *my son*? The beach disappears into black water when the river bends left, and the swamp takes over again.

A swallowtail kite hovers above the boat, at the height of the tree line. I haven't seen one of those since I was a kid. I don't believe in omens or signs, but with Thom lost on the river, I take any help I can get. Me or the bird—I can't tell who's trailing who at this point—maybe we're both following the river since it's the only thing that offers us a definite direction to move. I keep hollering Thom's name and waiting for a sound in return. Nothing. Just other birds tuning up deep in the swamp. That kite banks ahead of me on a funnel of warm air, then circles back, like he's scouting. If I had his altitude, I could see down the river, maybe get an idea of where Thom is. I hope he knows to pull over when he sees the hunting shack, *if* he sees the hunting shack.

How is Thom even steering that goddamn boat? Maybe, when I was running down the hill, the Old Man said something about a paddle being in the boat, but Thom doesn't know a paddle from a spatula. I haven't taught him anything. When was I supposed to show him how to paddle a boat? I only get him a few days out of so many. And he never takes those earbuds out of his ears. I don't think I've ever seen that kid—my *son*, I mean—without something plugged in his ears. Roma says constant sound in his head helps him focus. I think that's bullshit. It's just a way for him to ignore the rest of us. Every kid does that in one way or the other. What Thom wants isn't that different than any other kid. He just has an odd way of going about it.

I'm beginning to recall things. Like how to cut the paddle stroke in a J-shape, keeping this crooked boat straight in the channel without having to switch sides each couple of pulls. I pause the paddling only when I need to wipe the sweat streaming off my forehead. I'm making good time, but not as good as that bird above me. He's starting to get impatient with my progress, but I clip along, stopping only to yell Thom's name a few times. In fact, I'm starting to feel better, starting to think that he's all right. *He must be all right. If he weren't, the kite would let me know.*

The river here is wider, the current slow and steady. I round a sharp bend that splits into a small oxbow lake to my right. I should paddle into it, just to make sure Thom didn't get confused and steer off the channel. At the opening to the oxbow I spot something that makes my breath lodge in my throat. The thick top of a cypress has fallen into the river channel, blocking half of it, creating a huge strainer. I feel the current pick up, almost turning to white water, sucking me toward the downed cypress, where there's something thin and white in the wet branches.

Thom's earbuds, dangling like a taunt.

11

The first thing I need to do is avoid the strainer, so I back-paddle a few quick strokes and nose the crooked boat beside a cypress trunk, lodging me in a slower part of the current. With the paddle extended, I reach the earbuds and pluck them off the branches. *Maybe they aren't Thom's*, I think, trying to fool myself out of the terror that has crept up my throat. I don't know of many kids who would head downriver with earbuds plugged into a phone, but I could be wrong. I *need* to be wrong. I peer into the strainer, searching for another sign, hoping I don't spot a face staring at me wide-eyed from just under the surface. I can't breathe, and I think, *I'm drowning and I'm not even in the water.*

That's when he shows up.

That's when Lonnie Tisdale wedges his way into my head, the way he always does when you least want him to, when you least expect him. I was Thom's age when Lonnie Tisdale was supposed to meet me behind the elementary school, near that rusty soccer goal nobody used, because we didn't care anything about soccer back then. Thirteen, and Lonnie Tisdale never showed up and his mother ran door to door that afternoon, looking for her boy in all his usual haunts, but she didn't find him. Nobody found him that day. Or the next day either. It took three long days for the sheriff's department deputies to snag him out of the river with their hooks. He'd drifted a quarter mile from the bridge he'd jumped off. And now, he pops up in my head, like he's telling me, *You can look into that water all you want, but he won't be here. The river moves the things it steals from you. Just ask me.*

I shove the earbuds in my pocket and shake Lonnie Tisdale from my mind's eye, then dig deep with the paddle. Ahead of me, probably around the next bend, maybe a tenth of a mile or so, the kite hovers over the tree canopy, gliding in tight calligraphy above the river. But I can't watch him, because I need to keep my eye on the edge of the channel, looking for clues, for Thom. My breath is tight in my chest, and I think about calling Roma. Why I don't know. To apologize, maybe—but for what? Nothing has happened yet, nothing except a kid floating in a boat.

Don't get ahead of yourself, I think.

I learned a long time ago, if you want real trouble, put somebody in a place where they are a complete stranger. Put them where they don't belong. Thom's a stranger here, on this river. I was a stranger, too, the first hundred paddle strokes, but I'm making time now, gliding on the current. I scan the banks for the hunting shack. Probably too soon, but I still look. Not much in the way of banks, either. I peer into the edges of the swamp for my boy. What was he wearing? Of course, what he always wears: cargo shorts way too long for him and a black Star Wars T-shirt. It would be hard to spot that shirt back in the shadows of the cypress. I should be yelling more. Why am I not yelling?

"THOM!" I shout and wait, shout and wait, shout, "THOM!"

My best friend, Lonnie Tisdale, died in this river. At some point he sucked in a last gasp of air and got nothing but water, black river water clogging his lungs like motor oil. I've always wondered if Lonnie panicked, if he struggled to get to the surface. I shouldn't be thinking about those kinds of things, shouldn't be thinking about Lonnie Tisdale's last breath. Lonnie Tisdale isn't important now.

"THOM!" Wait and shout.

But how can I not? This river—you can't see what's two feet under the surface. It hides so much. I need to yell again, but I can't breathe. It's not like I constantly remember Lonnie Tisdale. I just never forget him. He always shows up, sooner or later.

I round the bend where the kite last hovered and notice the

bird has disappeared, not a sign of him, but when the bend straightens, I spot something on the far bank. A dock, and above the dock on the bluff, sits a hunting shack with a crumpled tin roof that looks as if it's about to cave in. On the edge of the sandy bluff stands my son, waving like he's been expecting me.

When I get close enough, I'm finally taking big, deep breaths, and trying not to cry or shout, and Thom yells down from above, "GUESS WHAT? I CHEATED DEATH, ELWIN!" At least that's what it sounds like. I don't see the Old Man's other boat at the rickety, rotting dock. I can tell Thom is soaking wet. He's spent time in the water. No boat. Wet son. I can't breathe again.

Thom and I never hug much. It's not my fault. I enjoy a good hug, but Thom normally keeps his distance, even with his mom. But after I tie off the jon boat and climb the steps and reach the top of the little bluff, I wrap my arms around him, pull him in close, feeling the chilly river water seep into my sweaty T-shirt.

"Elwin," he says, his muffled voice buried somewhere in my chest. "I'm trying to tell you how I cheated death. It's an excellent story. Release me!"

He squirms out of my arms. "I was lying in the bottom of Private's boat, and I fell fast asleep in what must have been only seconds, Elwin. Can you believe that? I would never have imagined I could fall asleep in the bottom of a boat so quickly, but sure enough, I closed my eyes and the next thing I know, when I open them up, the sky above me is moving. Not moving, you know, like the sky usually moves, but I was being pulled beneath it, so that's when I rose up and the dock was nowhere in sight. I was scared, Elwin, I must say."

When your son—the one who rarely tells you how he feels—says he was scared, it's enough to put a dent in your stomach. I want to hug him again, and he must sense it. He begins to back away, toward the hunting shack.

"Where is the boat?" I say.

"That's at the end of the story, Elwin. With all those stories you reel out, you should know that you cannot rush an ending. Anyway, I know better than to panic, especially in a boat," he says. I think, *Yes, he is indeed related to his grandfather. He already knows the dangers of panicking.* "So there I am, drifting aimlessly, and I notice this paddle in the bottom of the boat, and while I'm not familiar with paddling—which by the way, you were really moving on the water when you came around the bend, it looked as though you are quite familiar with paddling, I was watching—I decided I could figure it out, so when I reached for the paddle, well, Elwin, I tipped the boat over. But I hung on. I cheated death, undoubtedly."

Thom walks fast while he talks, and I trail behind him like a bird dog. "Can you tell me what *that* is, Elwin?" Thom points at the cleaning rack hunters use, a simple, gallows-looking frame where they hang deer while they gut and dress them. The dirt under the rack is stained dark from the blood of so many hunting seasons.

"I have no idea." I lie, because I don't want Thom distracted by the thought of dying deer. "Can you swim?"

"I've had swimming lessons, but I never practice. I assume swimming is like riding a bicycle—once you gain rudimentary knowledge, you never forget how to use it, but since I don't know how to ride a bike either, that whole analogy doesn't hold water. That's a joke, Elwin. It's funny because I was in the water, and I'm not sure how well I can swim." Thom waits for me to laugh, but I can't muster one up, not now.

"So, Elwin, I had the boat to cling to, so swimming wasn't really needed. Funny thing, my earbuds were still in my ears, but I suppose when I tipped the boat, the phone became disconnected, because it's at the bottom of the river now, so there we were, me and the boat, floating downstream, me with my earbuds in my ears, not connected to anything. That seems like some sort of metaphor."

I reach in my pocket and pull out the earbuds I found on

the strainer. Thom's eyes widen. "Elwin! How in the world?" He seems excited to see them, as if he's suddenly reconnected with an old friend.

"I found them in a strainer," I say, handing them toward Thom, but I see him reconsider things.

"Nope," he says, "they are tainted. Bad—what is the colloquialism?—juju. And I *knew* that thing was called a strainer. I remembered because of #15, that story about you and Private floating down the river and shooting squirrels from your boat. See, Elwin, I listen to those stories occasionally. Anyway, the boat and I were lured into a strainer, and I suppose that's where the earbuds met their fate. I wasn't sure. I was too busy trying to remember how to swim. I was cheating death, Elwin."

The thought of my son in a strainer sucks the breath out of me again. I keep telling myself over and over, *He's standing in front of you. He's okay. He's standing in front of you. He's talking. He's not dead.* Lonnie Tisdale threatens to break into our conversation. Maybe Lonnie Tisdale was trying to do the same thing—cheat death—and he lost.

"Elwin," Thom says, snapping me back, "do you want to know what I did? I used my brain, that's what I did. First, I had to untie the rope from the boat because that metal thing, the thing that obviously pulled away from the dock while I slept, I surmise, and sent me on this journey—what is it called, Elwin, that metal thing you put a loop around?"

"The cleat?"

"Yes, a cleat. Well, it was dragging like a tiny anchor and threatened to snag in the strainer, so I untied the rope. Then, Elwin, I decided that I wasn't going to let the water and the branches win, so I used the boat as a shield, and we bounced. We literally *bounced* off the strainer and there we were, back in the current, heading toward the ocean. I suppose you could say I was lucky, or you could say I was inventive. I prefer you go with inventive."

Thom sits on the single wooden step that leads into the

hunting shack. I see it bend, even from his slight weight. I'm afraid the whole shack might tumble down on him. "I was able to steer a little by kicking, Elwin. Again, inventive. I had no idea where the paddle was. Far downstream, I would imagine, on the way to the ocean. Anyway, I kicked and kicked, and we ended up here. I saw the dock and kicked toward it. There's a little ladder in the water at the end of the dock. Did you see that? The bad news is, when I climbed up the ladder, the boat kept going. I suppose it's long gone by now, belly up. That is how I cheated death. I should probably give my story a number. It's #1, obviously."

Without skipping a beat, Thom says, "Elwin, there is a cat sneaking up behind you. Did you bring it?"

12

I never know whether to believe Thom. Often he tells you things simply to gauge your reaction, like a kid's game of Made You Look. I don't fall for it this time. Then, something hairy winds its way between my legs. I jump back when I see a thin orange cat circling my shins, and of course, that scares the cat. He skips around the steps and into the dark crawl space under the hunting shack.

"I tried to warn you," Thom says. "Now look what you've done, Elwin."

From the line of shadows beneath the shack, the cat pokes his head into the light. He doesn't seem scared or distressed. Rather, he looks bored with the two of us. Thom clucks a couple of times with his teeth, and the cat slinks out from the crawl space and stretches his spine and his jaw. His teeth are the color of butter. I can't see his backside to tell if he's a male or female, but he doesn't have jowls that a lot of orange tomcats grow in the wild. He (or she) takes a couple of steps—not hesitant ones at all—toward Thom.

"Don't touch him," I say. I can't imagine me having to explain to Roma that Thom survived a drowning but got mauled by a cat the minute he was rescued. The cat's orange fur is matted in a few places, but he doesn't have that completely feral look. He's been eating well. When he reaches Thom, he butts his head against his wet size-seven Chuck Taylors, then licks the laces, like he's thirsty.

"He's fine, Elwin," Thom says, scratching him. I spot the jigsaw shapes of missing pieces along the bare edges of his ears. "He's friendly. He seems to know I survived death. We are compatriots, I think."

I wouldn't imagine cats living under a hunting shack at the edge of a swamp know the meaning of *compatriot.*

"He's purring," Thom says. "That's a positive thing, right? I don't have much experience with the animal world. Purring means happy, correct?"

The orange cat flops on his back and gives up his belly. Thom rubs his fingers through the thick fur. I want to ask him if he feels tits, but that's a weird thing to ask your son. Instead I say, "I was so scared. I thought you were in big trouble. I thought…" And I stop when I feel something bubbling up from my stomach and hanging in my throat again.

"There was a moment of trouble, Elwin, but it's gone now. I cheated death. I'll name him Willie Nelson," he says, and it dawns on me that Thom believes he is going to keep the cat. "He acts like he's stoned and he's orange and very relaxed. Willie Nelson it is."

Those moments—when your kid says something and you wonder, *How the hell did he come up with that?*—I suppose they happen to every parent. But this is my first time. I have no idea Thom knows Willie Nelson exists, that he even knows what stoned means. Then again, I'm clueless about what he listens to in those earbuds or what he does during the days I'm not around him. I've asked about his music before, but he never answers. Maybe he's a big Willie and Waylon fan. Maybe he's learned how to fire one up. What do I know? What I do know is, we can't take on a cat. Willie Nelson rolls to his feet and finds a patch of sunlight the cypress haven't filtered out and lies down in the warm spot.

"There's no way. He won't be happy with us," I say, but even I can hear what a lame effort that sounds like. We shouldn't have a cat around on this trip, but how do you tell a kid who just escaped drowning and climbed out of black water that he can't have an orange reward? Thom knows my heart isn't in it.

"Willie Nelson is happy wherever Willie Nelson goes, and he is going with us," he says, sounding like he gained a few years of wisdom on the river. "Speaking of going, I'm not sure I'm mentally prepared to step back in a boat. How are we supposed to return to Private's house?"

On cue, I hear the low rumble and squeaky springs of the Mercury floating through the cypress. In a few seconds, the car pulls into view, Linda behind the wheel, the Old Man pointing at us. Linda hits the brakes a little too hard and throws the Old Man forward. He shakes his head, then climbs slowly and carefully out of the door. He didn't bother to change. He's still in his hospital gown and slippers, still wearing his aviators and the Texaco hat. Willie Nelson barely looks up. Maybe he *is* stoned.

"I'm glad you didn't drown," he calls out to Thom. "That would have been a lot of death to deal with."

Thom begins to cry, and it surprises all of us, even Willie Nelson. I've never been around crying kids that much. Thom's only let it go a couple of times. But this sounds different.

Between sobs, he chokes out, "I lost your boat." Takes a couple of quick, wet breaths. "And the paddle and that piece of rope with the…" Thom nods in my direction.

"Cleat," I say.

The Old Man walks toward us, and a breeze catches the back end of his hospital gown, giving us a quick flash of flesh before it parachutes back down.

"We should search for it," Thom sobs.

"You know, I don't really need that boat anymore," and he sounds like he means it. "Somebody downriver will find it up against a tree and think they won the lottery. Make their day." Thom smiles when he hears that. The Old Man spots the cat figure-eighting around Thom's legs.

"Son, where did you find that? I don't trust swamp cats. They been living on field mice and snakes. They'll kill you in your sleep," he says.

Linda steps out of the Cougar. "Oh no," she says, "a cat. I don't enjoy cats."

"Keep back, sweetie," the Old Man says. "He's got that look in his eye."

Thom reaches down and picks up the cat, which immediately goes limp in his arms, like he's just discovered the most comfortable perch in the world. I'm willing to bet Thom has never held a cat before. I want to tell him that thing might be crawling with a half dozen kinds of bugs, but I don't get the chance.

"His name is Willie Nelson," Thom says. "We just met. He's orange and very relaxed."

"Pop the trunk, Linda," the Old Man says, and panic seeps into Thom's eyes along with the remainder of his tears.

Willie Nelson jumps out of Thom's arms and makes a streak toward Linda's side of the Cougar. Somehow, she manages to block him from jumping in the front seat, and he springs up and lands on the hood where he collapses again, then rolls on his back.

"You got to give him credit," the Old Man says. "You can't drive off with a cat laying on the top of your car. He's a smart one."

"I don't want a cat," Linda says.

"I don't think he's yours to begin with, sweetie," the Old Man says and winks at Thom. My son is smiling again. "Let's go home. Elwin, did you tie that jon boat up? You can come back later for it. Paddling that tanker upstream is too much to ask of anyone." He wheezes a bit, searching for new air.

Linda hasn't taken her eye off Willie Nelson, who rolls back and forth on the Mercury's hood. "I don't want a cat in my car. He could pee."

"I told you to pop the trunk."

"He could pee there too. Cat pee is forever," she says. "Maybe if we all get in the car, he'll leave."

I'm surprised Thom climbs in the back seat. That glaze of panic has left his eyes. It's as if he realizes something we don't.

Soon we're all inside the Cougar, which is hot with the windows closed. "Crank it up, honey," the Old Man says. "The engine will scare him off." But he's wrong. Willie Nelson seems interested in the sounds under his head. He cocks an ear toward the motor.

Thom reaches for a button on the door and presses it down. Before Linda can remind us that the window won't come back up if you lower it too far, Willie Nelson leaps up the windshield. I hear a couple of quick steps tap-dance across the roof, then the cat somehow jackknifes his way through the open back window and into Thom's lap.

"That was impressive," the Old Man says. "Even for a swamp cat."

Thom is smiling now. "You can't get cat pee out of anything," Linda says, and sighs the sigh of someone who has raised a white flag.

"Go slow," the Old Man says. "If you don't shake him up too much, we might be okay. By the way, Thom, I'm not sure that watch is waterproof. It still ticking?"

I'd forgotten about the watch. So has Thom. He stares at his wrist and studies the hands.

"Yes, Private, we are still counting down the minutes."

Willie Nelson purrs so loudly, the sound drowns out some of the Cougar's rumble. Your son drifts away, almost drowns, loses a boat, and the next thing you know, you have an orange cat making noises in a Mercury Cougar.

The cat does not pee in the car. He leaves Thom's lap, jumps into the back window ledge, stretches, and closes his eyes in the sun before Linda eases off the sand road and onto the highway.

Willie Nelson acts like he's where he always belonged, and I admit, I'm a little jealous of him.

13

At the Old Man's river house Linda parks the Cougar and says she is going to make some egg salad because it will calm her down. "I found some eggs tucked away. You need to eat," she tells the Old Man. "You look like a towel on a broomstick." She leaves us standing outside the car, but Willie Nelson doesn't budge from the back window. All I can think about is how to tell Roma, gently and calmly, that her son took a river cruise and cheated death. The Old Man sees I'm distracted and reads my mind the way, I guess, fathers can. He leans over and whispers in my ear. I smell Old Milwaukee on his breath, and his whiskers brush my cheek.

"You ain't obligated to tell her a thing. Just tell her he lost his phone and found a cat. She'll have so many questions about those two situations, you'll never have to get into the whole floating down the river."

Thom motions toward Willie Nelson, and the cat hops through the open window, then walks in a couple of quick circles, taking it all in. To a cat, the Old Man's house probably doesn't look all that different from a run-down hunting shack. Something with a roof near a river. He threads between Thom's legs again, and it seems like he's made his decision to stick around.

"They don't allow pets at the motel," I say.

"Maybe that little girl can help us," Thom says, with more desire in his voice than I would like. He reaches into the pocket of his cargo shorts and pulls out the title page where she wrote her name. His face falls. The page is wet and tissuey and tears when he tries to unfold it. "Her name is gone," he says.

"Lily Salters," I tell him, and his face brightens again.

"It's been a pleasure to meet you, Private," he says. "I do not think you will die today." He glances at his new wristwatch.

"I appreciate that, Nostradamus," the Old Man says, leaning against the Cougar. "You got any feelings one way or the other about tomorrow?" Thom smiles at him and walks ahead of us toward the house, the cat trailing him like it's on a leash. They angle into the yard that leads to the river.

"Don't go near the water," I say, thinking it may be unnecessary, but with Thom, you never know.

"Help me to my chair," the Old Man says. "I ain't good on uneven terrain." He holds his arm out like a bird's wing, and I steady him while we move toward the porch. It's the first time I've touched the Old Man in a decade and a half. His arm is brittle inside the hospital gown. His aviator shades hide his eyes again, so I don't know if walking pains him or not.

"I don't really want to lie to Roma," I say. "Something bad could have happened." I'm hoping Thom isn't listening. I hear him talking to Willie Nelson below the porch, in the thick grass that runs down to the dock, but I can't make out what he's saying.

"You're an idiot," the Old Man says, letting me ease him into his chair. "Did you and your brother suck lead paint when your momma wasn't looking? Nothing happened, smart guy. There's nothing to report. No lie to tell. You don't turn on the news at night to hear what *didn't* happen in world, do you? Keep it to yourself. Despite what you may have heard, omission ain't a sin, it's a talent. Everybody who's married has a folder of secrets they keep on file."

"We're not married," I say.

"Well then, I suspect you don't even need a folder," he says. "You can probably keep track in your head. It gets waaaay more complicated when you get married."

"You ought to put on some underwear," I say. Down at the river, a doughy, sunburned fellow wearing a straw hat floats by, pedaling a fancy fishing kayak, dragging a line along the bank, trying to pick up a redbreast on a slow troll.

"So, Linda called you," he says. "She didn't tell me anything about it. She likes to fix things."

"Maybe she's got a folder of her own," I say, proud of myself for the comeback. He doesn't blink.

"I hope so," he says. "We keep our distance. You know, she still has her own house in town, same house as always. She doesn't live out here. I got a hefty price tag on my love of being alone."

There is so much I don't know, so much that stays in the dark. Speaking of high prices, that's what you pay when you stay away for so long. Those big, valuable gaps in your knowledge. So many years when the river was still flowing along, and I was never around to see what rode with the current.

"I guess you want to talk about this," I say. "I guess we should."

"This?" he says, and plucks at his hospital gown. "I'm sick and dying. End of story, in a manner of speaking."

"No," I say, "I mean, me. Why I haven't stayed in touch, why I stayed away. That's what you want to know."

"Son," he says, dropping his glasses down his nose, so I can see his watery blue eyes, "I hate to break it to you, but you ain't exactly been on the top of the conversation list for a long, long time. You ain't even in the top ten. And I already know why you left." He pushes the glasses back in front of his eyes and turns to the water. "Tell me when I'm getting warm. You're one of those people who thinks the world gives a shit about you. You whine about all the crap rolling downhill right on top of you, you know, like your buddy taking a header off that bridge when you were a kid and your mother dying and your father trying to live his life the way he wants, and now you have a son who's set up camp on the outskirts of normal. And you think the world notices and is going to hand you some sort of combat pay for all your trials and tribulations. Hell, you're the worst kind of angry man—the kind who thinks the world owes him something. The world don't owe you jack shit. The world is a big place, and you're just one little person hanging on to it, and no matter where you run, you're still that little person just hanging on. Years ago I would've told you to suck it up and grow a pair, but you weren't around to listen. Now it's a little late. Question is, what are you gonna tell that boy of yours about the world?" The Old Man sucks in a deep breath and holds it for a couple of seconds. "Am I getting warm?"

I'm suddenly thirteen again, and my father is explaining how the gears of the world turn. Back then I listened, because I didn't have a choice. I figured he knew why things happened the way they did, why your best friend jumped off a bridge on purpose or why boys tossed rocks into our baseball field from their side of the tracks and split Cal Holmes's face open or why I had a crush on Laurice Reeves that ate up my insides. I had no choice but to believe him. Today I don't have to, but I can't decide how to tell my dying father that he's no longer the smartest man I know. There are parts of the story—of my story—that he's never heard, parts I've told no one.

Thom walks into view below us, Willie Nelson following right behind. I want to cry when I see my son, my living, breathing son. Linda shows up with a paper plate stacked with egg salad sandwiches on white bread and a second plate full of Ritz crackers. I notice my fingers are digging into the arm of the porch chair.

"I need to go to the store for you. You don't have any pickle relish or mustard. It ain't really egg salad without the condiments," she says, not realizing the conversation she's walked into. "Does Thom eat egg salad?"

"I have no idea," I say.

"Yep, I'm getting warm," the Old Man says, reaching for a sandwich. Linda seems comfortable not having a clue what the Old Man is talking about. "This is gonna tear my stomach up, but I've been craving some eggs. Who cares, right? Carpe diem and all that."

Turns out, Thom loves Linda's egg salad, especially spread on the crackers. He feeds some to Willie Nelson, until the Old

Man says that eggs give cats the farts, a fact that sends Thom into a fit of giggles.

"Fart jokes are never not funny," the Old Man says.

Linda gathers the plates and tells me she's heading back to town, reminding me again that I don't have a vehicle here. "I can run you back by the hospital," she says, and we both look at the Old Man. "I don't imagine they gave away your room yet."

"You ain't getting me in that car," he says. "I've spent my last night in a hospital." The mosquitoes are swarming in the sticky afternoon heat, and he swats at the air around his ears.

"Suit yourself," Linda says, "but I'm not staying out here. I guess I'll be back early tomorrow to check on you. I closed up the windows so the bugs won't fill your house. You okay for now?"

"For now," the Old Man says, looking straight at me. I feel like I should say something.

"I'll be back," I say and immediately realize how lifeless the words are.

"Yeah, well, we'll see. Heard that before," he says and turns toward the river. "Thom, you take care of that cat. What time you got?"

He glances down. "Six fifteen, Private," he says. "I'm glad it's waterproof."

"I'm glad you are too, son," he says. "Don't forget where I am."

And that's it. No fireworks on the porch, no big explanations about anything, no confessions. The whole ride back to the hospital, I'm thinking the only person who came away with anything of value is Thom. He got a new way to tell time. He picked up a cat.

The rest of us? We're pretty much where we started.

14

There's no ledge in the back window of my pickup where the new cat can stretch out, but Thom assures me that Willie Nelson will be comfortable, whether he's under the floor of a deer shack or in the window of a Mercury or under Thom's feet in the cab of my Chevy. Willie Nelson, Thom says, "is fine and dandy where he lands."

Thom is drying out. His clothes don't look damp. On his lap, he's spread out his little notebook and the page from Lily's *Great Expectations*. The pages in the notebook have begun to curl, and I can see that all of his notations are pretty much washed away. He keeps smoothing out Lily's page with his hand. It's odd to see Thom riding in a vehicle without earbuds in his ears. He talks more than usual. "Private is a nice man," he says. "I'm very glad I met him. He's not what I imagined, especially from all your stories, Elwin."

"He's okay," I say. "He's changed." We pull into the parking lot of The All Excellent Inn. Willie Nelson stretches his spine when I turn off the engine. "He doesn't even mind that you call him Private."

Though the sky has not yet turned completely dark, a pair of security lights shine across the back parking lot. They've begun to attract clouds of bugs and what looks to be a couple of bats feeding on them in frantic dives. "I'm not sure how to handle this," I say out loud, but not meaning to. "Marvin probably doesn't want a cat in his motel room. What are we supposed to feed him? I don't really want to feed him. If we do, we'll never get rid of him."

"Willie Nelson can take care of himself," Thom says, and I believe him. He rolls his window up.

"The menu may change since he's in town now. Things are

different on the river," I say, acting like I know something about cats. And rivers.

When I crack the truck's door, Willie Nelson spots an opening. He leaps through and zips across the parking lot, but he doesn't run far, only to the high, untended grass at the edge of the asphalt, in the direction of the railroad tracks. He is so orange, he glows in what's left of the evening light. I think the cat running off is going to send Thom into some kind of manic fit, but he smiles through the windshield and studies Willie Nelson. You never can predict how Thom's going to act or what he's going to say. It's like lighting a fuse and waiting for the firecracker to go off. You know it's *going* to happen, you just don't know *when*.

"He's cleaning himself," Thom says. At the border of the pavement, Willie Nelson contorts himself into crazy shapes, licking his fur.

"I'm scared if we go after him, he'll run off for good," I say. "What should we do?" You've reached a kind of milestone when you start asking your kid for advice. That ought to be a moment to enjoy, I suppose, or worry about.

"We should simply watch him, Elwin," Thom says. So we do. I have heard about hairballs, so I guess I know a bit about cats. Cleaning yourself and yakking up the aftereffects is a faulty system, if you ask me.

"You had me pretty worried, back on the river," I finally say. "I was mad at you. I was scared to death, and then I was mad again. I was all over the board. I kept imagining all sorts of things, all of them were worst-case scenarios. I don't know how to describe it."

"That's called aphasia, when you can't find the words you want," Thom says.

"I don't know what I would do if something bad happened," I say, and that's when I start to cry. Not sobbing like Thom did a couple of hours ago, but crying nonetheless, just some sniffles and a tear that slides down one cheek. It doesn't seem to bother

Thom because he's seen me cry before. I'm a big crier. Give me a reason, and I'll shed tears.

"None of us knows what we would do if something bad happened, because it didn't. We don't have to imagine. Imagination is a safety hazard, Elwin," Thom says. He sounds a lot like his grandfather.

We're not very good at this, the two of us discussing subjects that carry some weight. We haven't had much practice. I usually let things trail into silence until I get bailed out by some new sound that intrudes. If nothing else, I have learned *that* lesson—if you wait long enough, the world will interrupt you.

This time the interruption is provided by the tiny girl who bangs on Thom's window with the spine of her *Great Expectations*. I think I am the only one who yelps, because Thom doesn't seem to notice. He still has his eye on Willie Nelson, who runs into the thick grass between the motel and the tracks. Lily yells through the closed window, her voice as puny as she is: "My daddy saw a cat run out of your truck. He says no pets without a pet deposit. And a pet deposit is a lot."

Her face presses the window, like she's studying a pair of exotic fish in an aquarium. She is so close, through her glasses I see that one eye is a completely different color than the other. I wonder if Thom notices it too. He's pretty observant. What does it all mean—that I'm not worried about my son's cat, and I'm more interested in a little girl's eye color? She seems to be waiting for something. Lily Salters and her great expectations.

"We need to put some food by the door," Thom calls out, then lowers his voice to a whisper so quiet, I lean toward him to hear. "I can't go out there, Elwin. That girl scares me a bit. I don't know how to behave."

That's the moment I realize Thom has a crush on her. That makes me happy. It's something I can talk to him about. I've been there before.

"Her name is Lily. It's okay to call her by her name," I say.

"Lily Salters. You told me. I haven't forgotten." Thom doesn't turn toward the window, but no need. Lily has disappeared. She's made her announcement and headed for the motel office. I'm guessing she's reporting back to Marvin. Thom lets out a deep breath. "She indeed scares me," he says again.

Get used to it, son.

15

As the light drifts away beyond the tracks, there we are: Thom and me and the motel girl, Lily, sitting in lawn chairs outside of our room, with a paper plate of soft, smelly cat food on the cement walkway, trying to lure Willie Nelson out of the grass near the tracks. Lily says it's okay with her father if she's with us. She says he doesn't pay much mind to her because she isn't interested in working, and "if you aren't helping him, he leaves you to yourself. I find hospitality work boring." I haven't seen a mother yet, so I'm afraid to ask. Lily's *Great Expectations* sits in her lap like a paperweight holding her in place.

Thom has loosened up a tad, but he's still nowhere near himself. We sit in the silence, staring at the tracks, silent except when Thom makes some of his strange swallowing noises. I got no idea where Lily found the cat food. She showed up at the door with a short stack of cans in her hand. Maybe The All Excellent Inn has a stash of tuna Friskies on a shelf somewhere. She wrangled some chairs too. I'm completely clueless how this plan comes about—lawn chairs and paper plates and cat food. It's like it just happens. Lily Salters makes it happen. I'll say this for her, she seems to be one of those people who get things done. You wouldn't think somebody so tiny could stir up the world that much.

After she set up the chairs and opened the cat food, Thom was afraid to leave the room for a couple minutes, but he finally appeared and eased into a chair. After a half hour of us staring and listening to what sounds like a chorus of a thousand frogs buried in the grass—which leads me to think there must be water beyond the asphalt—Thom leans across me toward Lily and says, "You know, I feel like I should mention at the outset, I cheated death today."

Good opener, son, I think. *That'll get her attention.* Thom wants to tell her the story, that's clear. But I have to hand it to Lily. She doesn't so much as blink.

"Cats have nine lives. Maybe you do too."

Thom narrates the entire story in a couple of breaths, and when he hits the part about losing his phone, that's when my stomach does a guilty flip. I know Roma will be dialing in, checking on us, and when she doesn't find Thom, I'll be next on the list. Sure enough, I pull out my phone and see that I have missed five calls from her.

"I need to get in touch with your mother," I say when Thom pauses in his story. "She'll want to talk to you."

"Don't tell her about the cat," he says.

"I'm not telling her about anything," I say. "Except maybe that you dropped your phone in the river and that's why you're not answering her."

I duck inside the room, where it is so much cooler, and wait for Roma to pick up. She machine-guns questions at me, which is nothing unusual. When I have Thom with me, she expects things to go wrong. She's convinced nobody else can do her job, especially a part-timer like me.

"I tried calling Thom a dozen times. Straight to voicemail. What in the hell is going on? Is something wrong? What did you do? Is he okay?" she says.

I don't know whether it's the heat or the fact that we saw the Old Man or all that paddling I did in the afternoon, but I'm suddenly exhausted. The weight of the day presses on my shoulders. I figure what the hell. "Your son cheated death. He dropped his phone in the river when he fell out of a boat, and he drifted all the way to a hunting shack where they hang deer up and bleed them dry, but he escaped all the snakes, and he's out in a motel parking lot sitting in a lawn chair." It takes all my energy to spew the information. There's complete silence on Roma's end of the line.

Finally, she breaks it. "No, seriously, Elwin, what happened? Don't fuck with me." Sometimes making a person believe the god's honest truth is harder than coming up with a decent lie.

"He's fine," I say. "Actually, he dropped his phone in the toilet, and it wouldn't dry out. I forgot to call you and let you know. And Thom has been busy. He may have a girlfriend."

More silence, then, "A what?"

"You've heard of those, right? Girls who are friends." I'm enjoying this. I'm never the one pulling these kinds of levers in our conversations.

"You're serious, aren't you?"

"Her name is Lily."

"You haven't been there a day! He's thirteen, for god's sake," Roma says. "How does someone get a girlfriend in a day?"

"You were thirteen once, Roma. Relax. Lily likes books. She's reading Dickens," I say, like I'm trying to sell the idea of Lily to Thom's mother. I'm still enjoying myself. I rarely have moments like this with Roma.

"That does it," she says. "I never liked the idea of you taking Thom down there. Did you even see your father? You said he was dying, and that is the *only* reason I let you take my son there. That does it. I'm coming down there, and I'm picking him up. You can wait around as long as you want for…for whatever the hell is going to happen. I'm coming to get Thom."

"Don't do that, Roma. There's no need. I was just trying to convince you he's having fun. I mean, I *think* he is. He met the Old Man and they talked. It went fine. And he found a cat."

"A cat? He found a cat?! How does a thirteen-year-old find a cat in a town he's never been to?" I imagine Roma shaking her head at the phone. "Did you even think about rabies?"

"See? You've forgotten being thirteen. That's the prime age for locating strays," I say, trying to lighten things up.

"I'm coming down there. Tomorrow morning," which makes me wonder why not tonight? If she's so worried, what's stopping her from hitting the road right away? "There are only two hotels in town. I'll find you. You can't hide from me."

"Sleep on it, Roma," I say. "Everything is fine. You want to talk to him, right?" I don't wait for an answer as I walk through the door. Lily Salters and Thom are sitting right where they started, my empty lawn chair between them, the two of them staring intently into the edge of the light.

"It's your mother," I say, and Thom reaches for the phone without breaking his gaze on the grass.

"Look, Elwin," he whispers. "Willie Nelson has returned." He sounds like the anxious narrator of a nature documentary. He grabs the phone from me and says, "Mother, I can't talk now. Willie Nelson is coming out of the high grass," and he hits the button, hanging up on Roma.

Roma stops calling back when I don't answer a half dozen attempts. The three of us sit in the heat and bugs, watching Willie Nelson meander across the parking lot. He doesn't look any worse for wear when he finally hunches over the paper plate and begins scarfing down the food. I don't know if Roma will actually make the drive down here tomorrow to check on Thom. Anyway, I thought she was somewhere out of town, someplace that required those deposits she mentioned. To me, sounds like Roma is holed up in her house during her Independence Celebration. Maybe those suitcases in the hallway were empty.

I know better than to call her back, but I'd like to tell her one more time that Thom is doing just fine. He has a girl he's talking to, sort of. He has an animal that came out of nowhere and appears to enjoy hanging around him. He has cheated death. He's doing the things thirteen-year-old boys do. Most of them survive.

"I will discuss the pet deposit with my father," Lily Salters says, folding one of the lawn chairs and motioning for us to stand up too. I guess the evening is over. Lily Salters is in charge.

Thom opens the door, and Willie Nelson strolls into the room like he paid for it. Thom doesn't know whether to follow the cat or stay with the girl. His confusion turns him into a statue, and he stands, paralyzed.

Welcome to thirteen, I want to tell him. It doesn't get any easier.

16

I'm expecting another night of Thom's wall-rattling snores, but I'm wrong. With Willie Nelson stretched out at the end of Thom's sleeping bag, they both sleep like they are in comas. I swear, in the dark I hear their breathing sync up.

I doze off and on through the night. Each time I wake I stare at the ceiling or the window until my eyes get used to the dim light, until I get jealous of Thom's deep, steady breaths, and I squeeze my eyes shut and hear the clanky wheels in my brain spinning.

Roma is not one to make idle threats. On the other hand, she doesn't normally go places where she won't know a soul. It takes something special for her to venture out alone. That's how we met. All those years ago, she showed up by herself at The Cotton Bottom for karaoke night, but all us regulars knew that "karaoke night" was a harmless joke, harmless because only regulars ever showed up at The Cotton Bottom. Nobody got hurt because everybody was in on the joke. Between happy hour and midnight on Wednesday nights, somebody would ultimately scream, "Time for karaoke," and Raymond and his cousin, Ralph, would stand up at the bar and start doing their a cappella Johnny Cash duets. When they messed up the words (like singing, "I shot a man in Reno, just to watch him cry"), everybody got a free beer.

Roma was sitting at the bar by herself when Raymond and Ralph cranked up, and after a half dozen tunes, she leaned over to me and said, "So, there's no karaoke machine, is there?" I wanted to say something smart-ass, like "Can't sneak anything by you," but she was too pretty to make fun of—which I realize isn't a fair thing to say, but it's a fact. Pretty people avoid a lot of shit in the world.

She said her name was Roma, and I almost missed it because I was spending too much energy staring at her eyes. They were the green you usually see on exotic frogs or kids' watercolor paintings. Her hair, dark as chocolate, hung over one of the eyes, which I thought was a shame. *Those eyes need to stay where you can see both of them*, I thought. When I told her there was actually no karaoke and that the wrinkled flyer on the door advertising such was about five years old, she started throwing back Old Crow and crying. None of us at The Cotton Bottom knew what to do with a crying woman. In fact, most of us were there because of that very defect in our characters. Me asking "Why are you crying?" might have been the most obvious question, but it seemed to open other floodgates besides tears, and she told me that her therapist—"Not a real doctor so I can't get any pills or anything"—had suggested trying things that she'd always been afraid to attempt, but really, really wanted to do. "A bucket list of fears, you know?" she said between sobs and sips. Singing karaoke in a strange bar, she confessed, was near the top of that list. "To be honest, I'm afraid of singing in public *and* going into bars where nobody knows me. I can knock two things off the list in one shot. That's smart, right?"

I'm not sure getting picked up by an older man in a bar where they lie about karaoke night was on her list as well. She followed me back to my duplex where she started calling out things I didn't expect, right in the middle of the goings on. I thought it might be the Old Crow talking. And I don't mean she was talking dirty. She was chanting affirmations. Like, "I can accomplish whatever I set out to" and "I'm in charge of my own destiny" and "If I see it, I can do it." Over and over, between her short breaths.

Now that I think about it, those things she was saying might have carried a double meaning, especially when somebody yells them while she's astraddle you on a ratty couch in a cheap apartment.

The next morning I woke up as she was sneaking out. And

she was crying again. "I can't find my left shoe," she sobbed. "I'm always losing things. I'm not usually like this. This isn't me." Which is what people say when they are acting *exactly* like who they are. "How old are you anyway?" she said when she finally took a breath.

"Too old for karaoke," I answered, which I thought sounded witty.

"There's no reason to be mean," she said. I saw the toe of her missing shoe poking out from under the couch. A nice cork wedge with two straps, maybe a size six and a half. I thought about saying, *If I see it, I can do it*, but even I knew it was too soon for that brand of humor.

She spotted the shoe. "See? This is why I shouldn't go where I don't know anybody. I always end up meeting the wrong kind of person. No offense."

"Now who's being mean?" I said, but it didn't really bother me. My skin has grown relatively thick over the years. A perk of advancing age.

"Well," she said, slipping on the shoe. I couldn't look away from those eyes. "I am leaving. I probably have an appointment with my therapist. If I don't, I probably need to schedule one. Thank you for the evening."

"Next Wednesday," I said, "karaoke night." Maybe I sounded too happy, because that sent her into another round of tears when she passed through the door. I watched from behind the blinds as she climbed into her car. It was a nice one, a new Toyota, I think. I didn't realize somebody so young could be so messed up. She hadn't lived long enough to discover all her problems. *Maybe she was just an early bloomer,* I thought.

Roma didn't come back to The Cotton Bottom the next Wednesday or the one after that. It was eight Wednesdays later that she showed up again. I counted. She dragged me into the parking lot and told me she was pregnant but didn't shed a tear the entire time, like something had hardened in her head and in her backbone. She was all business. She was in charge of her own destiny. She's been that way ever since. I've never asked her if making a baby was on her bucket list of fearful things.

I run Roma's story over and over in my head and don't notice the sky lighten outside the window frame of room 113 and don't really register the sound of tires crunching the asphalt outside, headlights on and gleaming around the shade I'd pulled down hours before.

My first thought is that I have conjured up Roma. It's my fault. *Could she have gotten here this fast?* Then, after a meek tapping on the door, I hear Linda's voice seep across the threshold. She says, "I have news," and Willie Nelson snaps awake, like he sleeps with one ragged ear open.

17

Linda did all her crying on the way to The All Excellent Inn. She had her moment, and now it's gone. Her eyes are wide and rheumy, even in the half-light of the early morning. Lily Salters left two of the lawn chairs propped against the outside wall, so Linda and I sit facing the parking lot instead of each other.

"You ought to let that cat out," she says. "They have to pee in the mornings, just like people." I hadn't noticed the scratching behind me. I crack the door, and Willie Nelson slides through, then lumbers slowly across the parking lot to the tall grass. For such a thin cat, he's got a heavy walk. He looks back once as sort of a thank you.

I already know what Linda is going to say. She thinks it's going to be hard to tell me, by the way she fidgets in her chair. It's the particulars I don't know. She doesn't waste time with a drawn-out, dramatic announcement. She launches into the details. I appreciate that.

"I went by early to make him breakfast. That's what I do almost every morning before the sun comes up. He likes to eat a little something before it gets light, especially since he moved out to the river. He likes scrambled eggs with a dab of hot sauce. Eggs aren't the best thing for his stomach, but he does love them so."

The thought of the Old Man's eggs tugs at Linda's breath, and she pauses until she can move on. "He was still sitting on the porch. That's the saddest thing, I believe. I mean, we all knew he was going to pass. But the fact that he was sitting on the porch all through the night…all by himself, all them mosquito bites, all that dew falling down on him the whole time. He looked like he had measles, with all them bugs. And sometime during the night, his hospital gown blew up, so when I walked up, there he was, in his altogether. Mosquito bites everywhere. I covered him with a quilt and called Floyd's, and they came right away. They're good about that sort of thing."

Linda suspects she's done a poor job of telling me the Old Man is gone. I reach over and pat her on the shoulder because she probably needs it more than I do. I can't lie. I've imagined what I might feel when I find out the Old Man is dead. I've had practice losing things in my life. When my mother died I cried, because I was sad, of course, but also because I knew she'd just given up. She lived as long as she could with a husband who spent half his time hiding out in a decrepit shack on the river and the other half ranting about his usual list of complaints: a bad stomach, warm beer, shady politicians. Eli and I had directions we could run when our legs got strong enough, and the only time we came back was when she died. She deserved a goodbye. After we buried her Eli took off again, so far away, nobody knows where he is now. I still haven't figured out how someone can disappear in the world these days, but that's the way he wants it, I suppose. I didn't disappear. I just hung out on the edge of contact, far in the distance but close enough to keep an eye on the past. Maybe I was too scared to completely disappear.

And then there's Lonnie Tisdale. Another thing I lost. A friend who laughs one morning and drowns that afternoon. I was too young to understand how death skews time, how it doesn't care about schedules and clock hands. I was supposed to meet Lonnie Tisdale at four o'clock near that soccer net with the holes in it. Death didn't care we had a meeting. Neither did Lonnie.

At his funeral we had to put on our Little League baseball uniforms and sit in the church and watch him fade away right in front of our eyes. We were thirteen. You're not supposed to be in a baseball uniform and crying and wondering why your friend thought it was more important to jump off a bridge than meet you at the soccer field. I didn't run far the day of that funeral, only as far as the river. The Old Man helped me get there. But I ran much farther the first chance I got, the first time I was in charge of my own feet and my own compass.

Willie Nelson makes his way across the parking lot, stopping once to sniff the air and check for whatever it is that might be tailing him. He pauses at Linda's legs and sniffs them too. I wonder what he can pick up from just a couple of sniffs. Does he know that Linda has brought bad news? Does he sense somebody has died? He finds a space between the chairs and curls into a tight circle of fur.

I know I'm supposed to say something, but I can't bring it up. *He's in a better place. I'm sorry for your loss. He'll be missed.* I normally don't worry much about lying, but these fibs catch in my throat.

"It's their job," I say. "Floyd's is used to picking up bodies." Linda is disappointed, I can see. She expected more from me. Even Willie Nelson appears underwhelmed. My father dies, and I say something about the undertakers.

"I know y'all had your problems," she says, "but he wondered about you all the time, both you and your brother. He knows he failed you in a lot of ways. Maybe he should've said something about it."

And there you go—the regrets of dying. Running out of time for the things that mean the most. "It was complicated," I tell Linda, but she isn't buying it.

"Not really. Nothing is complicated if you look at it long enough. Y'all just never took time to study on it."

She's right, of course. But that would have required a different kind of energy. "What, exactly, killed him?" I say. "I'm not really sure anybody ever told me what was going on." I run through all the possibilities in my head: boredom, too much Old Milwaukee, guilt, some kind of crazy microbe in the river water.

"That stomach of his," she says. "So many operations all

them years ago. Not being able to eat the right kinds of things. That finally caught up to him. Took a while, but finally did."

The Old Man's Vietnam stomach. He caught some jungle parasite, and a military doctor in San Francisco cut away half his stomach and a big chunk of his colon. He hasn't enjoyed hard food since the early 70s. He used to tell me and Eli, *My last steak was Saigon.*

"It's been getting worse the last couple of years," she says, and again I have nothing in return. I'm not good at this.

The door behind us opens, and Thom sticks his head through. Willie Nelson cracks one eye to check out what is going on. For a split second, Thom seems happy to see Linda, then he recognizes he's interrupted a gray conversation. "Oh," he says. "So it has happened."

He looks at the watch on his wrist, his other hand patting the pockets of his shorts for his notebook, so he can make a note about the time. "I suppose this will affect us in different ways. That's something to think about." He opens the door wider and Willie Nelson retreats to the motel room. "So that's what I'm going to do, think about it," Thom says and closes the door.

Out of the mouths of goddamn babes. Or thirteen-year-olds.

Part II

The Shack

18

A funeral home is not a popular destination for a thirteen-year-old but leaving him alone in room 113 isn't much of an option either. And nobody knows what to do with Willie Nelson, who seems right at home in the room, with an occasional visit to his giant litter box near the railroad tracks.

Thom makes an argument to stay at the motel. "I'm thirteen, Elwin," he says. "What were you doing at thirteen?"

"You're not doing yourself any favors, comparing the two of us." When I was thirteen my parents left me at home during summer days while they were at work. My job was to watch Eli until my mom ended her shift at the hospital. We never admitted the things we got into—shooting expensive goldfish with our BB guns in the Goldens' algae-covered pond, tossing dirt clods at passing trains, riding our bikes across Highway 52 to the Bantam Chef to get some fries. Some stories are meant to die without proper confession, I suppose.

"Willie Nelson is not fit for traveling today," he says, which is not a revelation. Willie Nelson never looks fit—or interested—in anything that's going on. Thom keeps pushing. "We can't leave him here alone. And we can't take him in the truck because at some point we'd have to leave him in a hot vehicle. That's abuse, Elwin, plain and simple."

I lay down some rules. He must stay in the room. He can open the door only to let Willie Nelson out. If someone knocks, don't answer. Don't use the motel phone. (Not that he would know how. I'm pretty sure Thom has never dealt with a landline. And this phone is old. He would have to dial a number instead of punching it in.) As I recite my conditions, Thom makes tiny check marks in the air with his index finger. "Got it, Elwin," he says. "Got it."

I hustle across the road to the greasy, faded Huddle House and buy him some breakfast. He wants pancakes, but all they have are waffles, so when I tell him he'll have to make do, he says, "I can't negotiate all the little squares, Elwin. The strange geometry of it makes me anxious," and I wonder to myself, *How big of an idiot am I for leaving this kid on his own when waffles scare him?* Maybe this is how it happens—you throw your kid into the deep end of the pool and watch him swim toward shallow water as best he can. The last thing Thom says to me is, "You don't seem all that sad, Elwin, but it's okay if you're not, you know. You shouldn't feel guilty about it."

Linda never hears any of this. She sits in her Mercury with the AC going, waiting patiently. I wave at her when I half-trot to Huddle House, and she waves back like she understands exactly what's going on. When I'm finally ready, she rolls down the window.

"Sorry I took so long," I say. "Had to come up with a plan."

"Oh, honey, it's okay," she says. "Your father isn't going anywhere. Neither is Floyd's."

"Why don't I just follow you," I say. I recall the day before. I'm one of those people who don't like to be without their own vehicle. Or I guess you could say, without an escape route. She doesn't seem to mind.

Floyd's Funeral Home has been around as long as I can remember. It still sits, gleaming-white and looming—camouflaged in a copse of sagging oak trees—right in the middle of town, dripping with Southernness, with its long, deep porch and perfect white columns. Even the gravel spread on the driveway and the parking area is white.

In the front hall, a photo of the original owner, Asa Floyd, hangs in a spot you can't avoid. Black-and-white and softened around the edges, the picture has the feel of the 1960s, when Asa Floyd buried nearly everyone who passed away in Williamsburg County. His suit is perfect, the lapels in the photo so sharp, they might draw blood if I run my finger over them. That was the story I heard, even when I was a kid. Nobody ever saw Asa Floyd wearing anything but a well-pressed suit.

Linda catches me studying the photograph. "He died ten years or so ago," she said. "For some reason they had to take him all the way to Florence to get embalmed. Isn't that something? Not wanting to get embalmed in your own funeral home." Linda snickers like a gossiping schoolgirl. "His niece took it over a few months ago. She's a piece of work, that one."

As if Asa Floyd's niece has been summoned, an office door opens and out steps a woman with a hand already extended. "Linda, how are you dear?" she says. "I think we've got everything taken care of." This woman has not carried on the family tradition of a nicely pressed suit. She's wearing droopy overalls that have seen stiffer days, especially on the knees. The Panama hat on her head is looped under her chin with a string, and her shoes—probably a men's size nine—clop on the hardwood floors. Old-school brogans, unlaced, the tongues hanging forward as if her feet are gasping for air. She is a big woman. She owns the space she stands in. "Told you," Linda whispers out the side of her mouth.

"I'm Ruby Floyd," she says, her hand still leading the way. When I grab it, I feel hard labor in the skin, palms that handle a shovel or an axe on a regular basis. I can't imagine anyone developing calluses working with the dead. I wonder if she digs the gravesites, but that doesn't make sense. Ruby looks old-school, but not so much that she hacks out space in the ground for her own customers.

She says, "I'm sorry for your loss." But I can tell she doesn't mean it. "I'm supposed to say that. That's what they teach us in funeral-home school. There's a special class for it. Platitudes 101."

When I drop her hand, she spins and heads back toward the office, calling over her shoulder. "We have some paperwork and I have some questions, then we can take care of the business at hand." She turns around at the door. "Business at hand…that sounds a little harsh. Let me rephrase. We must attend to your loved one's final wishes. Platitudes 101." She disappears into the doorway.

Linda is at my shoulder. "Did I mention she sells real estate too?"

People keep telling me things, and I have nothing to say in return.

19

In Ruby Floyd's office, there is little to remind you that she deals with the dead. In one corner a stack of yard signs stands upright. *Another Fantastic Floyd Property!* they read, in large maroon letters. Maroon seems to be her color. It dominates the office. The picture frames on the wall, the lampshades, the curtains. The deep, soft redness gives her office the hint of an old school steakhouse. Her desk ought to have a white tablecloth covering it.

Inside the dozen or so maroon frames on the wall are photos of a wedding. Not the same one, but different weddings, all on the same porch, the porch of the funeral home. Ruby notices me staring.

"I'm trying to build up our event business. You know, weddings and anniversaries and things," she says. "Everybody gets a free portrait on the veranda." She gives the word *veranda* extra energy, shoving it out of her mouth.

"Interesting way to kick off a marriage," I say, "getting married at a funeral home."

"Hey, there's a lot more competition in the corpse business these days. I gotta do what I gotta do. Diversify. Multiple revenue streams. Sure, *everybody* dies, but not at the same time. But lots of people get married. How often are there anniversaries? How often are there reunions and birthdays? Every year, my friend," Ruby says. "I didn't get a business degree just to bury people. I can't make enough money to keep the farm going if I just wait around for folks to kick the bucket. And that wedding-dress store I opened died a horrible, expensive death. Please, sit." Ruby waves at the pair of chairs facing her desk. I notice the coasters there, emblazoned with a fancy chicken, a gamecock. Ruby Floyd is a graduate of the University of South Carolina.

The ubiquitous maroon suddenly makes sense. I am not sure *kick the bucket* is a phrase I want to hear at that moment. Ruby doesn't care. She plows ahead. I don't think Ruby cares about much, except which particular stream her revenue flows down.

"I have his suit in the car," Linda says. "I had to pick it up from my house. It's the only one he owns. Hasn't worn it in years, but I think it will fit fine for a funeral." I'm guessing the last time the Old Man wore his suit was when he buried my mother.

"Well, Linda, we don't really have to worry about a suit," Ruby says. "You didn't happen to notice the piece of paper, did you?"

Linda shakes her head. I'm falling behind and afraid to catch up: Linda grabbing a suit from her closet, pieces of mysterious paperwork…These people seem to know what to do when someone dies.

"It was on his wrist," Ruby says, "a rubber band holding it there. I guess he wanted to make sure he didn't drop it."

"Well, I did see something on his wrist, but I didn't want to touch anything," Linda says. "All I did was put a quilt over him, and that was because of the bugs."

"You've been watching too much TV, Linda. It wasn't a crime scene. He'd rubber-banded his will to his wrist. Looked like a cheap corsage. It's a copy, but it had a notary seal on it and everything. Anyway, he wanted to be cremated. No burial. And he had some specific things he wanted done with the ashes. And with his hip joint."

I haven't reacted properly to anything that has happened this morning. I feel like I'm straddling the middle stripe of a highway and cars keep whizzing by on each side. Nobody is stopping to pick me up. Nobody stopping to catch me up.

"Hip joint?" I ask.

Linda sounds a little perturbed that she has to answer. "Your father had a hip replacement a couple of years ago," she says. "You didn't hear about that?" She knows the answer to that question, so it feels a little mean-spirited of her to even ask it. She must be getting tired.

"He wants you to have it," Ruby says to me. "Listen, I'm no lawyer, and a lawyer usually tells you all these things, but, yes, he wants you to have his old hip joint. He knew it wouldn't burn up when he was cremated. He called me about it."

"You talked to him?" Linda says, jealousy shading her question.

"A couple of months ago. He asked how much it would cost to cremate a body and have the cremains prepared. He was very specific. And he seemed to have a sense of when it would happen," Ruby says.

I don't know if *cremains* is a real word or something Ruby Floyd made up for the ashy tributary that feeds her funeral home revenue stream.

"He said you'd know what to do with the hip," she continues. "Oh, and he doesn't want an urn for the ashes or a service or a memorial or anything. I don't think he was trying to cut costs. He just wasn't all that interested. Some people like it bare bones." Ruby presses her hand to her mouth. "Dammit. Sorry."

Ruby reaches across her large, maroon-tinged desk. "Here's the copy of the will. I don't think there's anything keeping me from giving it to you. I mean, it was on his arm with a rubber band." She folds the sheet of paper in half and lays the will down in front of us. Linda leans back in her chair, as if to say, *I don't want any part of that.* So, it's left to me. I put it in my shirt pocket without taking a look.

"What happens now?"

"Nothing really," Ruby says. "He paid the bill in advance. I'll take care of the departed, and you can come back in a couple days for the baggies."

"Baggies? Good lord…" Linda says, her voice pitching into a near-falsetto.

"Just read the will," Ruby Floyd says. "It's all in there. Pretty dadgum clear, I gotta say. It seems like he was a very careful man. He told me what to do with the ashes and everything."

I don't have the energy or desire to argue with Ruby. Careful is not a word anyone ever associated with the Old Man, at least not in my memory.

"Baggies?" Linda says again, and Ruby points at my shirt pocket. I think she is done talking, but she surprises me.

"Elwin, I have a couple of things I'd like to discuss with you," she says. "But it can wait until the dust settles. Again, probably the wrong thing to say right now. Jesus, I've got to do better with my timing."

Ruby stands and wipes her hands up the front of her overalls, then steps toward the door. "I'm assuming you'll want to see him before we start the cremation process. Say goodbye?"

I barely said hello, I want to tell Ruby, but she doesn't wait for any answers and disappears into the hall. Ruby Floyd is used to having people follow her.

Linda sniffles. "I've already done that, on the porch," she says. "But maybe you ought to. Get some closure. I think I'll head for home."

I've never known what closure is. Feels to me like the Old Man has already closed everything. Linda sniffles again, and I wonder why I'm not more struck by his death. Too many other things zipping around in my head. Is Thom okay back at the motel? What am I going to do with a cat? How many nights can I afford to stay at The All Excellent Inn? I have no idea how long this will take and no idea what I'm going to do with baggies full of human ashes. I reach for my shirt pocket but decide this is not the right time to read the Old Man's will.

Ruby sticks her head through the door. "Is anybody coming?" she asks and disappears again. Linda waves at me. "I'll be fine. I'll wait here for you."

I didn't realize how tall Ruby Floyd is the first time we walked down her hallway. Her unlaced brogans don't have much of a heel, and she could still almost look me in the eye. It's hard to put a finger on her age. I'd guess maybe forties, but overalls tend to make folks look older than they are.

"We don't put makeup on the deceased we plan to cremate, so he'll be like Linda found him." She pauses in the hall. "I'm sorry if I'm not too good with the empathy. I've only been doing this a short while, and I still haven't got the hang of dealing with the dead. The living are no piece of cake either."

"My father and I haven't seen much of each other lately. Actually, that's a lie. I haven't seen him in years. The only reason I'm back here now is because Linda called me. I left Kingstree a long time ago. I wasn't sure I'd ever be back. I'm not sure how this all happened," I say, finding myself suddenly revealing too much to a complete stranger in overalls.

"I have learned this so far," Ruby says, leaning in like she's going to confess. "Dying does strange things to the living. It never makes sense. Somebody is suddenly gone, and the ones left behind start doing things and saying things that feel brand new. It's weird physics. Every death is an action, and all we can do is create a reaction. I see it every day. Well, not every day. Every day would be good for business. But I see it often."

Ruby takes a breath, but she's not finished. She gathers herself. "So I guess what I'm saying is, whatever you're feeling, you're not that special. It's been felt before. Somewhere else in the world today, there's a son getting ready to say goodbye to a stranger who happens to be his daddy."

I follow her into a large, sterile room, lined with glass-fronted cabinets. Three long tables occupy the center of the room, and on the middle one the Old Man lies face up, his body covered not by a quilt, but a clean white sheet pulled taut around him. Dead, he looks even thinner.

"The mosquitoes did a number on him last night," Ruby says. Linda had already prepared me for that. He indeed looks like he might have died of a severe case of the measles, his bare cheeks dotted with dozens of welts.

The soft light shines down on him and fogs the edges of his features, but I can see he has the beginnings of a smile on his lips, almost a smirk. The expression has a soundtrack. I hear him saying, *I knew you'd be here. I knew all of this was going to happen.*

"What did he die of?" I say. "Linda said it was something about that stomach of his, but that's sort of random."

"Oh, I'm not sure. Linda told me he'd been sick a long time. Cancer, maybe?" Ruby says. "But you know, does it really matter? Do you really need the specifics? I mean, what difference would they make?"

It would be hard to tell Ruby Floyd that I want to know if something actually killed the Old Man, if something won. Or if he just let himself go. A quiet sort of suicide that left a smile on his face. "No, I guess it doesn't," I say.

"In the obituary, just write *after a long illness.* That's what folks always put down. Unless it was a short illness. Then that's what they say."

An obituary. I hadn't thought of that. I guess I'm the one who should write it. Maybe Linda could take care of it. I wouldn't know what to say. I can't think of anyone who would care what I wrote about the Old Man. Eli might. I should try and call Eli. Maybe Linda has a number. I don't.

"I'll leave you here for a few minutes. We aren't cremating until this afternoon. That's when Stanley comes in."

I wonder if they recruit Stanley from out of town. "I'm good," I say. "I don't need any time. Like I said, we never talked that much."

"Suit yourself," Ruby says, then sighs heavily. "Sorry. What I think I'm supposed to say is, 'Are you sure? This is your last chance to make your goodbyes.'"

I suddenly regret not bringing Thom. He would have something to say to the Old Man, because he is the kind of kid who has no trouble filling up blank spaces. I should call the motel, make sure he's okay. "No thanks," I say. "You know, the last thing I said to him was 'I'll be back.' I think that's what I said. So here I am. I'm back."

"The world is a circle," she says. "We all go back to where we started at some point or another."

Ruby Floyd could be smarter than she lets on.

20

Seeing my dead father makes me want to talk to my living son. I dial Thom's iPhone, and the call goes straight to voicemail, which jostles me into remembering that his phone currently lies in the sandy muck at the bottom of Black River. I punch in the number for The All Excellent Inn before I make it back to the car. Marvin must be on a break because there's no answer until the sixth or so ring. I'm hoping Thom knows what to do when the ancient phone rings in room 113. He's never had to pick up a phone attached to a cord. One of the rules was not to use the phone in the room. I'm hoping Thom can't resist the ringing.

Marvin connects me, and I let the phone in our room ring for thirty seconds, fear creeping into me when Thom doesn't answer. When I call Marvin back, he says, "I connected you, for sure. The phone works, man." Marvin's voice is pure Lowcountry, thick with Cedar Swamp or Sandy Bay, flavored with hints of stretched-out Gullah vowels.

"I know," I say, "but Thom didn't answer."

"Oh," Marvin says. "That's all because he's not in the room."

"Jesus, Marvin, you could have told me that!"

"You didn't ask," Marvin says with a drowsy calm in his voice, suggesting I'm not the first person to yell at him over the phone. "He went with Lily and that cat to the pool. I gave you a break on the pet deposit because of Lily, you know. Sometimes that girl isn't good for business."

"The pool?" I'm talking loudly. I didn't know The All Excellent Inn had a pool. I don't want Thom near any more water during this trip. I still don't know if he can swim. He can hang onto a capsized boat—that's been established.

"Didn't you read the brochure?" Marvin says. "We got a pool on the far side of the motel. Now, it doesn't have any water in it, but it's still a pool. You can't catch me for false advertising. They are just sitting there. I checked five minutes ago. The cat is in the deep end, lying down at the drain."

I try to imagine Thom and Lily, lounging like vacationing adults, poolside in their folding chairs while their cat slides down the slope to the deep end of a big cement hole. There is something grown up and sad about the image that flitters into my brain—sad because Thom is changing, and I'm never a spectator for the important moments. But I have an excuse for this particular one, and it's lying on the stainless-steel table in Floyd's Funeral Home.

I crank the truck, and Marvin breaks back in. "But don't worry," he says, "they aren't alone. Your daughter is out there with them."

That stops me from reaching for the gearshift. I'm confused only for a second. Of course I have no daughter, but I do have someone who could pass for one.

"Roma," I say, not really to Marvin but more to the air.

"That her name? What kind of name is that?" Marvin says. "She told me she was looking for her son Thom and his grandfather. I thought you said he was your son. Maybe I heard wrong. I don't listen to people all that close sometimes."

This isn't the time to explain to Marvin that I got mixed up with a woman who was in charge of her own destiny, and the two of us are doing the best we can with a third human that we made. I could also tell him that Roma has a sense of humor that maybe six people in the world understand. I don't care enough about Marvin to fill in all the blanks I'm hearing on the other end of the line.

"I guess there could be some funny business is going on," Marvin says, "but y'all look like decent enough people. I'm a pretty good judge of folks. Comes with the territory." That, I think, and the fact that we are paying for more than one night. Cash in hand trumps funny business a hundred percent of the time.

I pull around to the southwest side of The All Excellent

Inn, the farthest point from room 113. Just as Marvin reported, Thom and Lily flank Roma, the three of them kicked back in chairs. Roma wears huge sunglasses with bright white frames and a pair of neon-yellow sandals. Her shorts are hitched up a little so she can get some sun, even though the sun is barely over the trees yet. They each have a drink in front of them, with what appears to be little umbrellas sticking out of the tops. I don't see Roma's car anywhere. She waves when I get out of the truck, a bit too enthusiastically, I think.

"Well, look who decided to show up and check on things back at the ranch," Roma says, and Lily snickers. She may have been inducted into that small club of humans who think Roma is funny. Thom stares intensely at the empty pool, like a lifeguard on duty, his eyes locked on Willie Nelson. "So much has happened," Roma says. "Pets, new friends..." She tips her drink at Lily. "River excursions."

"Not now," I say. "Not a good time. I was at the funeral home." It's bad form for Roma to climb up in my business when I've just left Floyd's. But the second I say it, I can tell she knows nothing about the Old Man being found dead on his deck at the river.

"The what?" she says and immediately turns to Thom. "You didn't say a word about that." Her voice sings with a sharpness I have never heard her use with Thom. Almost like she's saying, *I can excuse a lot of things because of your spectrum, but you left me out to dry on this one.*

"You never asked," Thom says. "You just assumed the worst. You're comfortable with that." Thom doesn't break his gaze from the empty pool.

"Elwin, I didn't know," she says, standing up. I can tell she wants to give me a hug. "Are you okay? Is there anything I can do?"

I stand there, trying to decide which Roma is real: the one who leads a motel owner to think I'm her father or the one who offers to help me out when my own father dies. Maybe she's both. That would make more sense.

"I'm okay," I say. "He's going to be cremated." I don't know why I added that piece of information.

"That surprises me," Roma says. "I can't say why, exactly. I didn't really know the man."

"Well, of course," I say. "I mean, how much can you really find out from a few phone conversations?" I hadn't planned on lobbing that one at her so soon. But it's always nice to have information nobody knows you picked up along the way. Lily and Thom lean forward in their chairs to watch Willie Nelson make his way up the slope of the deep end. The pool has been dry so long, there's no algae or scum on the bottom. They aren't listening to us. They rise from their chairs at the same time, as if they received instructions the rest of us can't hear.

"Don't make a big deal about it," Roma says. I can tell she's afraid Thom is too close to the edge of the pool. "I called him occasionally to remind him he has a grandson. I knew you weren't taking care of it. He seems like a nice guy. Seemed. Sorry." Roma wants to move the conversation in a different direction. The sun that was rising behind the trees goes dim when thick, dark clouds slide in front of it. The temperature is dropping quickly. I've stopped sweating.

"Is there a service or anything?" Roma says. "I didn't really bring clothes for a memorial." Odd, I think, that Roma believes she would belong at a memorial service for the Old Man.

"You probably couldn't pick this up from talking to him on the phone, but he isn't a memorial kind of person. He left some instructions." I remember the folded piece of paper in my front pocket. The wind picks up in the tops of the pines.

"Willie Nelson is nervous," Thom calls out from the pool's edge.

"I think it's the weather," Lily says. There must be a set of steps in the shallow end of the pool, because half of Lily Salters disappears as she eases down a couple of them. She begins calling Willie Nelson in this pretty, lilting chant. It doesn't even sound like English.

"Don't you go down in there, Thom," Roma says, and I'm

almost ecstatic when Thom ignores her and climbs into the pool.

"No earbuds, and he still doesn't listen," Roma says. "Back to your father." As if the mention of him conjures something harsh in nature, a blast of lightning sizzles behind the pines, striking on the far side of the tracks. Before the thunder answers, Willie Nelson streaks past us, his legs moving faster than I thought they were capable. Thom scrambles out of the pool, and I'm about to yell at him not to leave Lily, but he's already reaching for her, extending his arm over the edge of the shallow end. He pulls her up the steps, and the two of them run in the direction of Willie Nelson, who has vanished.

That's when the first sheet of rain unleashes from the sky above The All Excellent Inn, huge drops that splatter the cement of the pool deck. Thom and Lily disappear around the corner of the motel, and I start to run after them, then realize Roma isn't following me. When I turn around, I see her standing still and upright, staring at all of us scrambling away from her. She doesn't appear confused. More bemused than anything else. She's in the process of getting soaked.

"There's too much going on," she says and begins laughing, her face turned up toward the storm. "What am I doing here?" I don't have an answer for her, at least not one I can come up with in the pouring rain.

21

We stand dripping in the lobby of The All Excellent Inn, and Marvin isn't happy. "You're going to be the one who mops this up," he says to his daughter, like she's a miniature employee. Rainwater dots the lenses of her glasses.

"We'll take care of it, Marvin," I say, and add, "I'm not a grandfather."

"Look, y'all need to leave here. I could have other customers. I can't have wet people in my lobby." He glances toward the door, as if to greet this band of mythical customers. The rain hammers the parking lot on the other side of it. Mixed with the smell of wet humans is another odor I recognize. Then it hits me. Marvin is stoned out of his mind. He'd been firing one up in the office when the rain hit. *I don't really blame you, Marvin*, I think. I suddenly feel closer to Marvin, not because I want to join him, but because he's another guy looking for a way to handle his little world. I decide to help him out. There's a breezeway that can get us close to room 113, then an awning the rest of the way that will cut the rain.

"We'll head to our room, Marvin. Lily can come too," I say. I'm not sure what he makes of us—a kid who is suddenly all goo-goo eyed for his daughter, a grandfather who isn't a grandfather, a woman who might (or might not) be the mother of my child. But he doesn't protest, which lets me know that he's happier getting high than he is being a parent. Again, can't blame him.

"We lost Willie Nelson," Thom says, panic squeaking into his voice.

"He handled a lot of storms in the swamp. He'll figure it out," I say.

"The swamp?" I can never predict what will catch Roma's

attention. "The cat is feral? Holy shit, Elwin." She claps her hand over her mouth. "Sorry," she says behind it.

"It's cool," Marvin says. He reaches behind the counter and grabs a small stack of hand towels. "Here, these will help." He smiles at me, and we suddenly have some sort of pact between us.

A couple of minutes later, we've made our way through the storm, and we're drying off inside room 113, but Thom insists we leave the door open. "Lily and I need to watch for Willie Nelson," he says, like the two of them have become a special team that accomplishes tasks together. *Oh, son*, I want to say, *careful. It's like that empty pool. You start sliding toward the deep end, there won't be a thing anybody can do for you.*

The rain blows by in thick sheets, and the sound funnels through the open door. Every so often I feel soft spray from the storm. I think about changing shirts—the one I have on is still plastered to my skin—and the thought of the Old Man's will floods in like more rain. "Dammit," I say and reach for my pocket. The sheet of paper is soaking wet, and I unfold it carefully, like an archeologist with a fresh artifact, then spread it on the small bedside table.

"Nice," Roma says. "I hope that wasn't important."

Thom and Lily perch in the doorway on a single desk chair, their heads close together, scanning the parking lot for any sign of Willie Nelson in the deluge. That cat has found some place dry and warm, probably a long way from here, but I don't want to say anything. No need to disappoint them. I haven't seen them speak more than a dozen words to each other. Instead of talking, Lily and Thom constantly appear to be on the lookout for something, the two of them on a joint mission.

The Old Man's last will and testament begins to dry in the light from the bedside lamp. I didn't know he could type. I feel the Braille-like bumps of the official notary seal under my finger.

"Geez," Roma says. "It's his will."

"Yeah, the funeral person had it. I suppose he knew she'd

be the one I talked to. I'm starting to think he had this whole thing planned out."

"Put that away. I don't want Thom to see it," Roma says. "He's too young to be dealing with a will."

If you count up the days over the course of Thom's life, I haven't spent many of them around Roma. Our face-to-face encounters are pretty much limited to picking up Thom and dropping him off. But I have noticed that she protects him from the strangest things, things you wouldn't expect. She'll let him cross the street by himself and walk down to the little QuickStop store in their neighborhood, but she won't let him watch National Geographic specials because he might see an animal die. She doesn't care if he sits in a doorway during a thunderstorm, with a little girl he barely talks to, but she's worried that a piece of paper from a dead grandfather could scar him forever. Maybe if I were around Thom more, I'd have to make decisions like that—what to be concerned about and what to let ride. Or maybe it's just that Roma is too busy trying to turn Thom into somebody new, she forgets to notice who he really is. I feel guilty I don't have the chance to make those decisions.

Thom calls over his shoulder, startling Roma and me. "I have no interest in Private's effects."

"Private?" Roma says.

"I'll explain it to you later," I say, but I'm thinking, *Does it really surprise you that Thom would make up a strange name for his grandfather?*

I can't remember the last time I read something that actually rolled out of a typewriter. This must have been an old machine. A dozen of the keys were dirty because the letters smudge and spread in their spaces. The *h* is completely missing.

Roma lowers her head near mine, into the light. Her lips move as she scans the lines. I never knew she does that when she reads.

So ere's w at I want you to do. T ey tell me t e ip joint won't burn up so once t ey fis it out Ruby says s e will give it to you and you can do w atever you want wit it. I don't really care. I didn't want it in t e first place. I told Ruby to divide up t e as es into six little baggies you know t e kind t at t ey use for sandwic es or w atever. S e can figure t at out. Anyway, I want you and w en I say you I mean Elwin to get in t e jon boat and start at Bakers. Between Bakers and t e s ack t ere are four bends in t e river. Dump a bag at Bakers. T en dump a bag of me out at every bend and watc me float away t en go to t e next bend. Dump t e last baggie off t e dock at t e s ack.

Roma finishes the first paragraph about the same time I do. "Seems a little gross," she says. That catches Thom's attention. He tilts his head in our direction, his eyes still trained on the sheets of rain dancing across the parking lot. Room 113 is beginning to feel musty and thick with the smell of the storm. I put my finger to my lips and nod toward Thom. Roma gives me a thumbs-up, which seems a bit too dramatic. We start on the next paragraph. I suppose the comma key is missing too. I haven't seen one yet.

Speaking of t e s ack I leave it all to you Elwin for w at it's wort . I got no idea w ere Eli ended up so I can't leave anyt ing to somebody w o don't exist and t at all makes me sad. Your mot er would be sad too but I won't get into t at. We all did a lot to make t at woman sad. I wasn't t e only suspect in t at particular crime. Anyway Elwin came back so e gets t e s ack and t e land and all t e stuff inside except for t e canister above t e fridge wit t e c icken ead on top. T at goes to Linda. Anyway you probably oug t to go t roug it and take w at you don't want to t e dump. T at's pretty muc all I ave t at land on t e river and it mig t be wort somet ing to somebody. It was wort a lot to me. Got a pretty good return on t at investment.

"I never thought I'd miss an h so much," Roma says.

"He probably did it on purpose," I say. It would be just like him. Do just a little something to push you off balance and make you forget you're hearing from a dead man. Above the raised seal and all of the signatures is one final line. Roma and I see it at the same time.

Last t ing w en you get on t e river and dump t ose baggies I want you to take my grandson wit you no matter w at is mot er says.

"Oh no," Roma says. "*That* is not happening. Nossir. He can't do that."

Before I start the argument with her, I notice the date on the will. The Old Man wrote it a year ago, wrote it while he was peering into everyone's future.

22

The rain hammers the parking lot for nearly an hour, then like someone flips a switch, the sun blasts through what's left of the clouds, and the whole world changes. Steam rises from the puddles in the asphalt. The smell inside the room alters, the mustiness evaporating like the rainwater outside. Willie Nelson strolls in, flops on the floor, and waits for somebody to rub his dry belly. He's not even damp. I wonder where he rode out the storm? Lily says that she needs to make some progress on her *Great Expectations* and heads in the direction of the lobby, leaving Thom with a blank expression of fresh disappointment on his face. Roma asks if he wants to watch TV in her room.

"I'm right next door," she says, flashing me a grin. "Wasn't that nice of Marvin?" The two of them walk the ten feet to room 115, Willie Nelson weaving toward their heels, and I'm left to myself. I suppose everyone needs a break.

I want to remind Roma that, technically, it's still my visitation with Thom, and if he wants to watch television, I have one too, but I'm not even sure it works. Come to think of it, I don't believe I've ever seen Thom watching TV. But it's not worth stirring up a mini-custody battle on the sidewalk between rooms 113 and 115. Like I said, the world has changed. The storm is over. Somebody died.

I can't stay in the room, though. It begins to close in on me, even with everybody gone. The door to 115 is open slightly, but I knock anyway.

"I have to run an errand," I say through the crack.

"I'm sure you have things to do," Roma calls out from inside. "With your dad and all." I am lying about an errand, but I indeed have things to do. The Old Man's jon boat is still tied to the dock at the deer hunting shack—at least I hope it is.

Hard rain makes high water, and high water does strange things. Also, according to an official notarized will, I'm supposed to go through his stuff and get rid of what nobody wants. So maybe I do have errands.

"You should lock the door," I say.

Thom answers this time. "Willie Nelson will need an option for exiting. His breed is very unpredictable." My son has become an authority on cats. I pull the door closed anyway. An open motel room door feels like the worst kind of invitation.

I stop by the Food Lion and buy a box of heavy-duty trash bags for the Old Man's shack. I probably won't need the whole box. The place isn't that big, but I know how things can accumulate when you live on your own. The road to the deer hunting camp is a thick, sandy soup after the rain, and I come close to losing the back end of the truck a couple of times, but I finally make it to the river. I had lashed the Old Man's boat tight to the dock on a couple of rusty cleats, so I'm not worried about it being there. What I hadn't planned on was a few inches of rain in an hour or so. The boat cocks to the side, half submerged. The soup can the Old Man mentioned yesterday must have floated away, and I can't find a bucket to bail with, so it takes me half an hour to splash enough water out of the boat to get it floating right, then another half hour to get it on the dock and tug it up the hill to my truck. I'm sweating and muddy when I finally head to the Old Man's place.

Being in need of a shower always puts me in a bad mood, so when I pull around the curve in the Old Man's narrow drive, I'm not happy to see a car parked there. I don't want people around. The old Ford Bronco seems familiar. It's parked so out in the open, I don't feel as though somebody's trying to rob the Old Man's place. Even so, I reach under my seat for my sawed-off Louisville Slugger, a Manny Ramirez model I cut right in the center of the trademark. I've never so much as waved it at anybody, but it's nice to know it's always there. I wait at the end of the driveway, blocking anybody's escape route when I remember where I've seen that Bronco before, and my fingers relax on the bat. Ruby Floyd appears around the corner of the shack, walking like she owns the place, and waves with both hands, as if to say, *Nothing going on here. It's just me.* I instantly imagine something's gone wrong. Maybe she is supposed to cremate some of his things along with him. Maybe he's not really dead. Maybe it's been a mistake or a dream.

Then it hits me: Ruby Floyd sells real estate. Ruby Floyd is working. It's borderline brilliant if you think about it. She has a fast track on property that will more than likely be hitting the market, since she buries most of the people in the city limits and a good many of the ones out in the county, like the Old Man. Ruby Floyd plays insider trading with the dead.

She's already talking when I pull behind the Bronco, and I don't even have the window down. She's ditched the overalls for jeans and a T-shirt, but she still clomps around in her unlaced (now muddy) brogans, still peers out from under the brim of her Panama hat. I catch her in mid-sentence.

"…another day or so. It only takes a few hours, but then we have to process the cremains." There's that word again. This time, it sounds like something you put in coffee. Ruby doesn't take breaths when she talks. "You don't really want that hip joint, right? I'll sterilize it for you, in case you change your mind. I thought I'd take a look at the place, maybe see if you wanted to list it. You've heard about Charleston, right?"

A strange question to ask somebody who grew up so close to the coast. Of course, I've heard of Charleston. But that's not what she's asking. She doesn't wait for my answer.

"It's the great climate change migration. That's really a thing, you know what I'm saying?" Ruby leans so close to the window, she's almost in the cab of the truck. She glances toward the road, checking to see if someone is sneaking up on us. "You see," she says, her voice lowering to a conspiratorial whisper. "Nobody is building beach houses anymore. Those people, the ones who have money, they didn't get rich being idiots. Okay, that's a lie. Some of them are mouth breathers that get their money because they are born into it. But the smart ones, they aren't sinking money on the coast because the coast is washing away. High tide is getting higher every season."

Ruby is exaggerating, I think, but she's trying to make a point. I pull on the door handle to let her know I want to get out, but she doesn't take the hint. She leans a few more inches forward, and I think Ruby Floyd has been to happy hour already. A wave of something—bourbon maybe?—floats into the cab. I'm not one to judge. I'm muddy and tired and could use a drink myself.

"So the one thing you need to know about people who have money is that most of them want to spend it, and if they aren't building beach houses, there's only one direction to go." Ruby eases out of the window. "And you know what direction that is, don't you?" I don't. It's not something I think about—rich people and where they waste their money.

"They come upriver because, you see, water is the common denominator. They want to be on the water, but they don't want high tide in their living room. All these people who used to build beach houses are looking for river property. And they aren't afraid to pay for it. The market is expanding and the inventory is limited."

I'm tired, so I'm slow. It takes me a second to realize Ruby Floyd has me in the crosshairs of a sales pitch. She leans back in, following a fresh wave of bourbon breath.

"You stand to make a good deal of money on this piece of property, Elwin. You've got access from the highway. Electricity is already run. You've got riverfront. Your father's property is a rich person's wet dream. So to speak."

I'm not expecting the sales pitch to veer in that direction. I can't imagine somebody with a stack of cash having nocturnal emissions about three boggy acres of swamp.

"I know, I know," Ruby says, "it's maybe too early to talk about selling the place. Your father just passed away. But I know y'all weren't all that close. You might not want to do anything to this place other than sell. Just remember, if you do, I'm your man. Let me help you with that boat. From the looks of it, y'all already wrestled once, and you lost."

Ruby hoists one end of the crooked jon boat, and we carry it down to the grass patch in front of the dock. There must have been a ton of rain upstream, because from the looks of things, the river is still rising on the Old Man's marks on the cypress. Nothing serious, but there's a lot of water moving downstream to the coast, toward the wealthy.

"I came to go through some of his things," I say to Ruby. "I figured I might as well get that done."

"I'll leave you to it," she says, and I start to ask her if she might have a flask in her Bronco but hold back. Having a drink would mean she'd stay around, and I want to be alone when I start filling up trash bags.

Ruby leaves me at the screen door. "Think about what I said. No pressure, of course. There's a whole bunch of those folks moving this way." She laughs. "They're like salmon, swimming upstream, going against the current, no matter what. Salmon with lots of money in their pockets." She laughs again. "I'll give you a call when you can pick up the bags of ashes. Are you really going to paddle to all those bends in the river and scatter the cremains? That's a nice father-son thing to do."

I've come to learn that Ruby Floyd doesn't have much use for back-and-forth conversations, so I'm not surprised when she turns and heads for her Bronco without waiting for my thoughts on the subject. I wonder if she is good at what she does. You'd think hearing what folks have to say is part of her job—whether it's burying people or selling the land the dead leave behind. But what do I know?

23

I'm not prepared for the emptiness of his tiny house. I stand in the crooked doorway, studying the single large room like a golfer surveying a putt, looking from every possible angle. When Thom and I were on the porch yesterday, I didn't so much as glance through the windows. I had been too intent on watching the Old Man and my son. The lack of awareness brings on a sudden wave of guilt. If I'd noticed how cleared out the shack was, I might have suspected the Old Man's passing was next on his horizon.

I can't imagine life this way. A single small dining table in the center of the room—a couple of cushionless chairs on either side of it. A shelf hangs on the wall and holds what looks to be a couple of plates and a single coffee mug. When I get closer, I see he stole the mug from a Waffle House. Against the far wall there's a cot covered with a quilt I recognize. My grandmother stitched it years ago. A faded yellow square from my mother's Girl Scout uniform makes up a corner of the quilt. I know it's there without picking it up. The floor is swept clean, and the shack doesn't smell like anything—nothing that suggests mold or bacon or spilled beer. That surprises me. Yesterday I'd caught a whiff of cooking. Maybe when somebody dies, they take their smells with them. He knew I would look in the fridge, because it's empty, other than a six-pack of Old Milwaukee with a handwritten note taped to one of the cans. *I figured this might be some kind of memorial after all*, it says.

I think about Linda and the egg salad she made, but the fridge is bare. No mayo or eggs or bread. I still have his will in my shirt pocket, so I pull it out and reread it, just to make sure I didn't misunderstand something.

Anyway Elwin came back so e gets t e s ack and t e land and all t e stuff inside except for t e canister above t e fridge wit t e c icken ead on top. T at goes to Linda. Anyway you probably oug t to go t roug it and take w at you don't want to t e dump. T at's pretty muc all I ave t at land on t e river and it mig t be wort somet ing to somebody. It was wort a lot to me. Got a pretty good return on t at investment.

Bastard. The Old Man couldn't die until I showed up, until he had a few words with his grandson. He mapped out the whole thing. Of course, he couldn't have predicted Thom taking an unexpected cruise downstream, but that didn't disrupt his plan too much. He cleaned the shack of everything he *didn't* want me to see and left the rest on top of the dining room table, like a museum exhibit.

I break one of the Old Milwaukees away from the plastic and sit down. The bare overhead bulb bathes the table in a sick yellow glow. I glance around for any other lights, but that's the only one. On the table sits a stack of pictures, most of them black and whites, all of them unframed. They're in no particular order, so time gets jumbled when I leaf through them. There's a photo of the Old Man and my mother, probably when they were dating. The expression on his face dares anyone to look at my mother the wrong way, a sneer of superiority and ownership and pride. There are photos of me and Eli I've never seen before. We are on a camping trip, obviously on the river, the two of us crouched like baseball catchers on a bright white sand bar. Another of me smiling, wearing my Kingstree Manufacturing baseball uniform—the teeth that aren't missing point in the wrong directions. A photo of my mother propped against the hood of a bullet-shaped Ford Falcon, and I see beauty and hope beaming from her face. I almost don't recognize the pictures of my father before Vietnam, before that parasite hitchhiked in his stomach and ruined the rest of his life, as far as eating was concerned. In those photos he's big and soft, like a risen loaf of bread. At the bottom of the stack is another one I'd never seen before. He probably wanted me to find it last. It's the Old Man and me and Lonnie Tisdale. Lonnie and I each hold a full stringer of hand-sized redbreast, our free arms wrapped around the Old Man's waist. He rests a hand on our heads. I remember that afternoon. It was the summer Lonnie dove off the bridge the first time. I know because his glass eye—the replacement for the one he lost when he banged his head on the submerged Kenmore refrigerator—is focused in the wrong direction, like he's spotted something nobody else can see. Maybe his glass eye was already spying the future, when he would take a second dive off Baker's Bridge, the leap that killed him.

I cried for Lonnie Tisdale years ago, at his funeral. For weeks afterward too. Cried a few times since, usually in the summer. But this time I cry for the Old Man. He's right. This is a memorial: me, sitting at a lonely table, shuffling through the past like a sad poker dealer, wondering where those days went, when young boys were alive and caught more fish than they could eat, and smiled at the camera while someone patted them on the head. Where did they all go?

I stop crying about the time I finish the second beer. I'll keep all the photographs. I need them. They capture time in a way I can't through sheer memory and imagination and random flashes of something that happened years ago. But I need to finish what I came here for—to clean the shack of the Old Man.

Other little piles line up on the table. Inside a purple velvet Crown Royal bag, I find his dog tags from Vietnam. I expect to see *Protestant* or *Methodist* in the space for religion. Instead, the Old Man somehow had them stamp *Nunya.* Did he convince somebody that was a religion? It's a word I'd heard a thousand times growing up. When I was a kid and the Old Man was making one of his exits out the back door—before I knew about his river refuge—I'd ask where he was going, and he'd say, "Nunya business." I guess that was his way of telling the army to keep their nose out of his spiritual affairs. The Old Man never had much time or desire for religion. Sure, there were the Easters when he played Jesus in the Easter pageants that Miss Burch directed. She liked the fact that he was gaunt and bearded. She told the Old Man once that he was born to play Jesus, and he told her she was liable get struck by lightning for blasphemy such as that. A tiny specimen bottle rolls out of the Crown Royal bag, the cylinder-shaped kind people use to collect bugs. It's empty, but ringed by the stain of a faint waterline, as if at one time, the bottle held some liquid. A minute dark speck—maybe dirt?—sits in the bottom. On a square of ancient, weathered masking tape across the cap, I make out the faded word *Cong*, I think, but the second word has survived the years. *Parasite*, it reads.

In a small stack of papers I find the deed to the land the shack sits on, along with the most recent electric bill. There's a short letter to my mother, written when he was in Vietnam, where he tells her how he doesn't want to die in a place he doesn't recognize, surrounded by people he doesn't really like. *That's the goddamn worst way to go,* he writes.

Sitting by itself on the corner of the table is a tiny square of toilet paper wrapped around his wedding ring. There's an inscription inside the circle. The formal cursive writing says, *Damn fine day*, and I have to confess, that makes me smile. Who cares about the date or love or promises? Having a damn fine day is something to take note of.

Finally, there's an envelope facing down. When I turn it over, I see my name written in the Old Man's minute block printing, my full name: Elwin Hayes McClennon. The flyer inside makes no sense—a cartoon of a dancing pig and a date that passed half a decade ago. I wonder why the Old Man has left me an old flyer for the Kingstree BBQ Cookoff, but then I turn it over and see he's composed me a note. Words fill every blank space on the bright yellow paper—top to bottom, margin to margin and they swim in the harsh light from the single bulb. I read it to myself, but I can hear his voice.

> I don't know what I'm supposed to say but I'm going to give it a go. I was never mad at you for taking off like you did and not coming back until you absolutely had to. I would have done the same thing if I had grown up the way you and Eli did. I'm not sorry about that but I am in an understanding of it. Linda has been in my ear for years that I should sit down and talk to you because Linda is one of those people who think talking about something will make it better. What Linda does not understand is that keeping your mouth shut is most times a sign of a strong person. Plus if we was to talk about me and your momma and all those times and you and Lonnie Tisdale and that bridge all we would do is wind up interrupting one another. That's the risk of talking. Sometimes nobody listens. I loved your momma and I can say that because I know about love. Here's something to take with you, the only way to know about love is to see it from all sides. That means you got to fall into it and fall out of it and get your heart broke. And break somebody elses because when you do that you'll know what it all means. You can't know it all until you hurt somebody. So now I know. I love you, boy. I know that for a fact because I've loved you from all sides. It's time for you to stop being one of those people who blame the past for your shittyass present. Stop blaming me. Stop blaming your momma. Stop blaming Lonnie Tisdale. He's the one who jumped. You stayed dry. You got a boy of your own. Tell him what he needs to know. Thank you for coming back. I knew you would. Make sure Ruby gives you those bags of ashes. Also it wasn't that goddamn Vietnam bug that finally killed me. It was just old age. I'm tired. I want some rest.

I hear a laugh at the end of his note, and I turn my head to make sure someone isn't in the shack with me. I don't know why I imagine the Old Man laughing at the end of a letter like this. I never know how to take the Old Man.

When my phone vibrates on the tabletop, I jump, jolted by the sound. It's Roma's number. I immediately think something has happened to Thom. Somehow he got back in the river and turned over another boat. Or disappeared into the tall grass near the railroad tracks, chasing after Willie Nelson.

I don't bother with a hello. "What's wrong with Thom?" I say.

"Where do I start?" Roma answers.

There isn't a hint of panic in her voice, but something lurks there, some tiny agitation. "That's not very nice," I say.

"I can say that. I'm the mother." That sounds like a line the Old Man might have written on the back of a BBQ flyer. I want to remind her that I'm the father, but she jumps in before I can speak. "Are you in the middle of something? I know your father just died, but we have a situation here."

"What? What's wrong?"

"You may not know this, but your son doesn't have much of a filter. He tells me everything, and sometimes, there are things I don't need to know. It seems that his new friend Lily wants him to kiss her. She just out and out asked him, like they need to schedule it."

"Lily?" I say, not able to imagine Lily Salters even knowing what a kiss is.

"Yes, you remember her, right? Tiny little thing, always carrying a book, stalking my son like a middle school vampire? Anyway, he wants me to tell him how to kiss. That, Elwin, is not something a mother is supposed to teach her son. Anyway, who gets kissing lessons? I mean, you just—I don't know—you just kiss. You need to come and talk to your son."

Roma waits and the silence hisses slightly. I can hear the Old Man talking again. *You got a boy of your own.*

"I'm on the way," I tell Roma. "Tell Thom not to go kissing anybody until I get back."

I got a boy of my own.

24

Thom waits for me outside room 113, sitting upright in one of the lawn chairs, Willie Nelson spiraling his shins. The empty chair beside him waits on me, I suppose. When I turn off the truck, Roma pokes her head from the next room.

"I mean, I know how to kiss, but I'm not an instructor," she says and closes the door. Thom doesn't seem fazed by the fact that people talk about kissing in front of him. There's no sign of middle school embarrassment. Any remnants of the storm are gone. The parking lot is almost completely dry. Only the deepest potholes still have water in them. The sun is beginning to disappear behind the far side of the motel. I wonder how many days Roma booked her room? Marvin is probably so happy he has a couple of multi-day tenants, he rolled a giant joint and celebrated in a cloud of smoke, a little happy storm of his own.

Despite what the Old Man wrote, I'm not sure keeping your mouth shut is the sign of a strong person. Me, I've learned that buttoning your lip is the cowardly way out, when you don't know what to say. It's got nothing to do with strength. Plus, this is Thom's conversation—or at least his topic—so I sit down and wait, the quiet coward.

"It's a conundrum," he finally says, his voice easing toward a whisper, like we are trying to keep a secret from somebody.

"How so?"

"Well, Lily and I walked into the grass to look for Willie Nelson. He made another escape for the railroad tracks after you left. I, of course, had become curious as to why he is so attracted to the tall grass. So is Lily. We are intrigued by the same things," he says.

What was Roma thinking, letting Thom off on his own? She has no idea about this part of the world. Snakes hide in the high grass. God knows what else. I've conveniently forgotten that Thom floated down Black River alone, on my watch. I should tell him: never walk where you can't see your feet. But I don't want to distract him.

"Suddenly, apropos of absolutely nothing, she asks me if I'd ever kissed a girl. So of course, I tell her, 'No, I'm thirteen,' and she says, 'Would you like to?'" Thom sighs, as if remembering the conversation bumps the needle on his anxiety.

"What did you say to her?" The best thing I can do now is ask leading questions. I'm in unknown territory.

Thom sighs again. "I ran out of the grass," he says. "I almost tripped over Willie Nelson. He was hiding from us, like a tiger. I don't know how to kiss anybody, Elwin. Like I said, a conundrum. I *want* to. But I don't know *how* to."

I remember my first kiss, from that McCutcheon girl. It happened behind the Youth Center during one of the Teen Canteen dances in the eighth grade. Only the brave and unashamed danced. The rest of us did laps around the edge of the big, open dance floor. I had a crush on Rachel McCutcheon large and powerful enough to leave me sleepless and tongue-tied for weeks. I rode my bike to her house at night and hid behind the Ligustrum hedges and tried to catch a glimpse of her in her bedroom window. I bought a Beatles record for her—a 45 rpm—and she refused the gift. At the dance, I was trying to recover from her in the only way an idiot kid knows how: by ignoring her in full view, by acting as if I enjoyed her rejection. That is, until I walked around the back of the Youth Center and found her alone and smoking a cigarette in the dark, the glow of it like some red-bulbed lighthouse, warning about the dangerous rocks ahead. I'd never seen someone my age smoking a cigarette. And that was when Rachel McCutcheon kissed me—when I got close enough to see her face. She didn't ask permission, like Lily Salters had done. She just did it. Leaned down (yes, I was shorter than Rachel) and put her mouth on mine. She tasted like smoke and strawberry lip gloss. For the next ten years, every time I kissed a girl, I thought of cigarettes. I hadn't received any instructions on kissing from the Old Man or my mother. The only advice he ever gave me about women was, "Keep it zipped until you know you're ready to use it." I hadn't listened to that closely enough. At least not with Roma. Hence, I have a son who wants kissing lessons. Fathers and sons. Shit keeps spinning in circles.

"Okay," I say. "The first thing is, you know she wants to kiss you. That's good. Because you can't go around kissing girls that don't want any part of it. That's wrong."

"That I know, Elwin," Thom says, releasing another sigh, this one spiked with exasperation.

"But you got to understand, there's no rule book. There are some things that just, you know, *happen.* And you need to do them wrong first, so you can learn to do them right later. Nobody knows how to kiss a girl the first time. You just sort of, I don't know, muddle through it somehow. Mess up, then fix it the next time."

Thom sits quietly for a couple of seconds. Then he shakes his head. "Elwin, that seems like an insane way to do *anything* in life."

I missed the moment when Thom magically evolved into a thirteen-year-old who talks like a college graduate. Maybe he is, indeed, on some kind of spectrum, one that allows him to skip whole chunks of growing up. He needs more Rachel McCutcheons in his life. Then again, maybe Lily is the newest version of a Rachel McCutcheon. Maybe these days the girls ask the boys *before* they lean down and blow smoke into their mouths. I suddenly feel every one of my years aching in my bones, bones aging instantly in a lawn chair.

"So you want details," I say.

"I want to know what Lily wants," he says, staring up at me like I have answers.

"Oh hell, son, you'll never know that. You won't know it now, and you'll never figure it out later. You got to learn to live with the mystery. That's part of the fun."

"That sounds horrendous," he says.

"You want to know how to kiss? Quit worrying about what she's thinking. Quit worrying about what you're thinking. Just don't think." I've told Thom to do something that he is completely incapable of. He knows it too, but he doesn't respond. Just releases another sigh.

"Close your eyes and let the whole thing unfold." *Unfold* may have been the wrong word, but it was the first one that crossed my tongue.

"Close your eyes?" Thom says. "That seems a little reckless...and haphazard. How do you aim?"

"Like I told you, that's part of the fun," I say. Thom smiles at me. It's not a completely foreign look for him, just a rare one.

"Thanks, Elwin," he says. "Eyes closed. Followed by the unfolding. I think I can do that." Thom pats me on the shoulder. "I feel better."

I catch sight of a crack in the blinds in room 115, and it suddenly vanishes. Roma has been watching us the whole time, grading me. I'm not sure how I've rated, but I didn't completely fail, and that's something to hang on to.

25

You are never prepared for the morning a funeral-home-director-slash-real-estate-agent arrives at your motel room door bearing a half dozen ziplock baggies of your father's ashes and his shiny, sterilized artificial hip joint.

Willie Nelson growls a low guttural rumble when he hears shoes scuffle on the sidewalk. I've never heard of a cat acting as a watchdog, and I think he's trying to protect us, which seems out of character for Willie Nelson. Thom spent the night in my room with his new cat, and he sleeps hard on the twin bed next to me, a leaf-sized stain of drool under his mouth. I believe the discussion about kissing wore him out.

I've already pulled on some shorts and a T-shirt by the time Ruby Floyd knocks quietly on room 113, and when I open the door she stands there, holding a small cardboard box top, six little bags lined up in two perfect rows, and presents them to me like an obsessive-compulsive drug dealer. She isn't wearing her Panama hat this early, but the brogans are once again unlaced. Yesterday's mud has been wiped away. I take a half-step over the threshold.

"I wasn't sure of your time frame," Ruby says, just above a whisper. She peers beyond me into the room and sees Thom sleeping. Willie Nelson has decided there is no imminent danger and flops on the floor behind my feet, waiting for somebody to rub his belly. "I thought I'd better run these out to you so you can complete all those final wishes and whatnot." Ruby grunts a little. "Sorry, *whatnot* is probably not a good word to use. Or maybe it's two words. Anyway, I wasn't sure how long you were in town."

"That's the joint," I say, pointing to the piece of steel lying behind the bags. It resembles an odd kitchen implement.

"Indeed it is." Ruby sounds proud of herself. "It's my first piece of surgical hardware to come through the oven. Probably not the last, what with the average age of folks around here. Lots of elderly walking around on fake joints and borrowed time. If you don't want it, I'll keep it as a souvenir." She laughs, and I catch something on her breath again. Not bourbon. This time it's breath mints layered over strong coffee. I suppose she thinks calling remnants of the departed *souvenirs* is okay.

"I'll take care of it," I say and reach for the box. Ruby pulls back slightly. She's holding the ashes hostage until she can say something else.

"Speaking of time frames, I know it's quick, but have you had a minute to think about what I said yesterday, at your father's? About your property? When it comes to these things, you have to strike while the iron's hot." She shakes her head. "Again, maybe not the best choice of words after a cremation, but what I mean to say is, I have a couple of interested parties."

"Some of those new carpetbaggers coming up from Charleston?" I say.

"That's a good one. The new carpetbaggers. Sounds like a band name." Ruby looks like she's getting tired of holding the box top. "So, any thoughts about selling the land? It's prime."

I catch a flick of movement in the periphery. It's Roma, peeking again through the window blinds next door. I never realized how much Roma likes spying on people. I completely understand. I was the same way when I was a kid. Lonnie Tisdale and I would hide in folks' bushes and peer into their houses after dark. It made us feel mysterious back then. These days, mystery is more of an annoyance than anything else.

Thom saves me from having to answer her question about the shack. When he speaks up from behind me, it startles both me and Ruby. "So that's what's left of him?" he says, rubbing both eyes with his fists. "That's not as much as I thought it would be."

"Good morning, youngster," Ruby says brightly. I see what

she's doing. If she makes friends with Thom, she might gain an ally in her run at the river property.

"How hot does the cremation oven get?" Thom says.

"He gets right to the point, doesn't he?" Ruby says, rolling the breath mint around her mouth.

"That's sort of his thing," I say.

"It's definitely my thing," Thom says and smiles at me, like we're on the same team. That's the second smile I've seen in less than a day.

"About eighteen hundred degrees," Ruby says.

"Fascinating," Thom says back, and I want to remind them that the Old Man is sitting right there, so to speak.

"What is *that*?" Thom says, his voice hitting a new pitch of excitement.

"He had a fake hip," I said. "Eighteen hundred degrees doesn't make much of a dent in…" I leave the sentence hanging because I don't know what hip joints are made of.

"Titanium," Ruby says.

"Can I hold it?" Thom says, already reaching for the box top. Ruby backs up again, keeping her grip on all the important things in front of us.

"Thom, I don't think that's—"

Ruby cuts me off. "It's fine. It's sterilized and cleaned up and everything." She balances the box top on her forearm, but when she removes the hip joint, it tips, and the bags flop to the sidewalk. We suck in our breath at the same time. The crack in the blinds widens, so Roma can watch what spills.

"Not to worry," Ruby says. "I used the heavy-duty kind." She picks up the half dozen parts of the Old Man and realigns them on the box top. Thom holds the hip joint to the sky, trying to catch some light on it. I'm sure Roma is not happy her son has a hip in his hand.

"Extremely bizarre," he says, "thinking this was inside somebody's body, that they were walking around on it. I need to show this to Lily. May I?" He looks up at me, waiting for permission. I guess he feels obligated to ask, since the joint belonged to the Old Man.

"Sure," I say. "If she's awake."

"She is," he says. "She told me what time she'd be at the front desk." He walks in the direction of the lobby, and he isn't wearing shoes. When you forget to put on your shoes, you got it bad. Crushes make you neglect your better habits, like dressing properly. Willie Nelson follows at his heels, more like a bird dog than a cat.

"You don't hear kids say *may I* much anymore," Ruby says, still trying to win points any way she can.

"I haven't thought about the property yet, Ruby," I say. "But when I do, I'll let you know." She crunches her breath mint, and despite her disappointment, hands over the box top of the Old Man's ashes and heads for her Bronco.

26

Roma is one of those get-her-way people, and a half hour later, she insists on coming with us on our cremains delivery expedition. Hell, I don't even want to take Thom, but the words from the Old Man's will (even the ones missing an h) still float in front of my eyes: *I want you to take my grandson wit you no matter w at is mot er says.*

The Old Man was worried about Roma trying to stop the trip. He never figured she would want to join it.

"I'm not sure we can get three people in the boat," I say. "Those things are tippy enough as it is," which is a stupid thing to bring up because it reminds her that Thom has already been in and under and hanging on to a Black River boat. But that boat is long gone. We'll have to take the cockeyed jon boat.

"All the more reason why I should be there—to keep you from drowning our son. Look, I'm small. Thom is small. We barely make up one adult between the two of us. We should be fine," she says, but she isn't completely convinced. Roma doesn't want anything to happen that she isn't a part of. She might even be jealous of me. I wonder if this is what a family feels like, everybody being weird about how time is divided up. Roma has something else on her mind as well. "Who was that woman in the fashionable footwear?" she adds.

"That was Ruby. She runs the funeral home," I say. "And she's a real estate agent. And she used to own a wedding store that went belly up because nobody wanted organic wedding dresses in Williamsburg County. She wants me to sell the river property." I probably shouldn't say that out loud because frankly, it isn't a real thing yet. Plus, I don't want Thom to hear it. I glance around to make sure he isn't eavesdropping, but don't see him anywhere in Roma's room. "Where is Thom?"

"I guess he's still with that Lily girl, showing her a prosthetic," Roma says, waving away my question with her quick answer. "Old Ruby sure didn't wait too long. Are you going to sell? What could you get for it? You could start a college fund for Thom, you know. We're probably too late to save for the total cost, the way tuition is these days, and scholarships are like the lottery. You just never know." Roma peppers sentences at me. Over her shoulder I see that she's been in the coffee that The All Excellent Inn provides. Three empty packets lie balled up on the table where the television sits. The smell of cheap coffee blankets the odors of cleaning supplies and mildewed carpet. Roma is wired.

"I think it's important that I go do this whole baggie thing with you. I mean, I've talked to your father more in the last couple of years than you have. I feel like he'd be okay with it, even though he didn't really mention me as a passenger," she says. "Would you like a cup of coffee? You see, I'm all out, but we could use yours." Roma's eyes are wide and bright, as if she's trying to see in a pitch-black room.

All the women I talk to lately seem to be drinking something to an excess. I don't think I'm to blame.

"Anyway, back to this boat thing. I want to be there," she says. "So, we can put a pin in that subject. I'm going and that's that." She gets out of the creaky wooden chair in the corner of her room and grabs the coffee pot and peers into the bottom to see if there's anything left, other than sludge. "When are we going? I need to leave tomorrow, so we should probably get going."

That's what I mean about get-their-way people. They don't know when to stop. Roma has already reserved herself a ticket in the Old Man's boat, and now she's making up the itinerary. Before I can answer, a flash of lightning flares beyond the trees across the railroad tracks. A couple seconds later, thunder rolls out an answer.

"We're not going anywhere," I say. "Not until this storm

passes. I should probably check what's behind it. If there's more on the way, we aren't going on the river today."

"Can I have a couple of your coffee packs?" she says. "I want a cup before we go get Thom. I don't want him running around in the rain with that girl." She sounds like that's a danger to avoid—girls in the rain.

I don't know where all these precautions come from. I've never seen the rule book.

27

The storm blows closer when we make our way to the motel lobby, the clouds over the parking lot turning thick and dark. Beneath the breezeway that skirts the asphalt, the smell of oncoming rain mingles with the odor of Roma's fresh cup of coffee.

Marvin's eyes barely flicker when we walk in. He stares through the front windows into the parking lot. "Storms are awesome," he says without glancing at us. "I love watching storms."

Roma is too hyped up to realize that Marvin is baked. "We're in that cycle," she says, suddenly turning into the local weather girl. "Summer storms that pop up out of nowhere then disappear. Unstable air. I hope this one doesn't last too long. It could, but maybe it won't. We can only hope. We have a boat trip to make."

"Well, I hope it lasts for hours," Marvin says. He and Roma peer through the glass. Another flash of lightning strikes in the distance, and seconds later, a long roll of thunder pays out. Marvin shakes his head in toked-up amazement, the two of them grinning at each other, like kids who both got the present they asked for.

"We're looking for Thom," I say, but neither of them breaks their gaze from the window. "Hey, Marvin!" I'm yelling now. "Thom? Lily?"

Marvin suddenly remembers he runs a motel, and a paying guest is asking him a question. "Oh yeah, they went to restock the soda machine. She has her own key." A kid with a key to a soda machine would be a modern Willy Wonka. I don't even know where the drink machine at The All Excellent Inn is located. I point toward the front door, and Marvin shakes his head.

"That way," he says, nodding toward the southeast corner of the motel. "Hey, man, would you mind taking this? They couldn't carry it when they left." Marvin walks behind the front desk and emerges with a case of Fresca. "This stuff is making a comeback," he says, like a stockbroker letting us in on a hot tip.

Roma leads the way as we head out a rear door toward the back of the motel. She keeps glancing up, expecting another thunderbolt any second. There hasn't been a drop of rain yet. The tops of the Fresca cans have little flecks of weed on them. Marvin must clean his pot over the cases of soda.

Roma stops talking when we reach the outside—all her attention is on the sky. At the end of the breezeway I see a little alcove, the kind of space that might hide ice and soda machines. "Over there," I say to Roma and steer her in that direction.

I am right—there's an ice machine ringed with rust, looking like it hasn't worked in years. Beside it, an antique Coke machine. The faded logo on the side looks like it's from the '70s. The heavy door is thrown open, a key dangling from the lock. The machine is loud, running hard to keep the cool air from escaping. A couple of empty cardboard soda cases lie scattered on the cement floor.

"That's not like Thom," Roma says, "leaving a job half done." I could argue that is *definitely* like Thom. It's like any thirteen-year-old. They have the attention spans of amoebas. The soda alcove smells like a wet dog.

Just as I put the case of Fresca on the ground—trying to decide if I should fill the empty slots in the machine—I see Willie Nelson bend into view around the corner of the building. Like Roma, he checks the skies and decides it's okay to brave the open space. A noise from the side of the building he just vacated catches his attention for a second, but he keeps walking.

"They must be over there," I say and head in Willie Nelson's direction. I have no idea why I peek around the corner. From instinct or habit or something I can't put a name on, I lean out slowly with one eye and sight down the wall. I feel Roma on my back. Maybe that's what parents do. When they sense they are about to witness something important, they slow down and poke their heads around whatever corner happens to be in the way. Or perhaps it's more human than that—that need we all possess to spy on somebody.

Whatever it is, when I focus around the edge of the wall of The All Excellent Inn, I see two kids standing on the ragged edge of the cement breezeway, where scattered grass has tried to pierce the cracks. A couple of soda cans sit on the ground at their feet, one of them on its side, a puddle of Sprite soaking into the walkway. Lily Salters and Thom face each other, with a narrow slice of space between them, like they don't want to get too close. In slow motion, tiny Lily rises on her toes, and my son bends forward at the waist, maintaining the blank space between them. Lily Salters reaches up and holds the side of his head—probably so she won't fall over—and the two of them press their faces together in a kiss so awkward, it resembles a bad cartoon.

I don't realize that I've thrown my arm behind me, blocking Roma. "Shhhh," I whisper. Roma wriggles under my elbow, then sticks her head around my waist and peers down the breezeway. I wait for her to react, to yell or hiss, but she's completely silent. The two of us crouch there, trying not to breathe.

I see Thom open his eyes, his lips still pressed to Lily's, but she has no intention of stopping, so he closes them again. We're watching a supremely rare event, like spotting an animal in the wild rumored for centuries to be extinct. I don't know how many parents witness their kid's first kiss. It *has* to be his first one. Only yesterday, he asked for an instruction manual.

Roma pulls back, out of sight, and whispers, "I feel guilty. Creepy too." A giggle lurks under her words. She quietly taps one of her feet, giving the caffeine energy an outlet other than her mouth.

I can't tear my eyes away. I think about Rachel McCutcheon again and suddenly sense cigarette smoke in my mouth. I wonder what Thom will remember about this one? Which details will he never forget? The thunder in the distance? The spilled soda can?

Thom's hands are buried in the pockets of his cargo shorts, and I want to call out and tell him that's probably the safest place to keep them for the next ten years or so, when he's making out with a girl. Roma reads my mind.

"He's not trying to cop a feel, is he? I can't watch," she says. "Tell me what he's doing." Suddenly, I'm doing play-by-play commentary on a kiss.

"No, he's not getting out of line," I whisper. "He's being nice. So is she. I don't know how she's keeping her balance."

It strikes me what a pure and simple moment this is. A pair of thirteen-year-olds who will probably never see each other after this week are carving an image into their brains that will last forever. That feeling of someone else's lips on yours for the first time. A gloom passes through me—mirrored maybe by the clouds rushing overhead—that Thom is also going to learn the harsh lesson of firsts. A first kiss happens only once. The feeling he's having this second will never be duplicated. There's a sad sort of realization that occurs only when he has kiss number two or four or twelve. He'll always try to retrieve that first feeling, and he'll always fail.

"What's going on?" Roma says.

"We have to leave," I say. "If we get caught, Thom will never forgive us." I back quietly away from the corner, careful not to scuff my shoes or kick something over. When I think we're out of earshot, I pick up the pace, and by the time we hit the lobby, Roma and I are almost jogging.

"Hey," Marvin says, perched on his stool behind the counter. "I think the rain is about to hit us. You find what those kids are up to?"

A streak of lightning flashes in the near west, which is a fortunate thing because Marvin is again mesmerized by the sky. Neither of us wants to answer his question, so we let it hang in the air, like just another cloud.

Part III

The River

28

The storm arrives in gray sheets of loud rain that fall the rest of the day, and as the sun dips below the tree line beyond the tracks, the sky breaks, and one of those crazy orange-pink sunsets seeps from the behind the remnants of the dark clouds.

Roma orders pizza, and we sit in room 115 and watch Thom eat. He hasn't said a word since he came back to the room. I hate the jagged silence of these situations—when I know something about somebody, and they don't have a clue I possess this secret knowledge. But that's the point of spying and make no mistake about it, that's what Roma and I were doing, spying on our son.

Once, when Thom goes to the bathroom, Roma leans toward me and whispers, "Are you going to ask him about it? I mean, what do you think he'll say?"

I don't have an answer, which is good, because Thom reappears and wants to know if we ordered garlic knots. The look on Roma's face mirrors what I'm thinking: Thom never eats like this. He's ravenous, and you don't work up this kind of appetite with just a kiss or two. Roma sighs, as if to ask, *What happened when we left the love birds by themselves?*

"You two are oddly quiet," Thom says, shoving the tip of a slice into his mouth. He smiles. I've quit counting the number of times my son has smiled in the last couple of days. It's becoming his new habit.

"My father just died," I say, thinking that will put a lid on any conversation. It's really an excuse to avoid interrogating Thom about his soda-fueled make-out session. Thom doesn't even tap the brakes for the conversational speed bump I lay down.

"It's not that kind of quiet," he says. "Not like you're experiencing grief. It's more like you're uncomfortable about something." Thom's either a mind reader or he's chumming the waters. I've got nothing; I played the dead father card, and it didn't quiet things down. Roma steps in.

"Your father and I had a discussion this afternoon, while you were out with…What is that little girl's name?" Roma says. My breath catches slightly. *God, she is going to tell our son we watched him kiss a girl behind a cheap motel.* And she damn well knows Lily's name. She's just looking for a tell on Thom's face when he has to say it out loud. My son doesn't flinch, and I'm proud of his poker face.

"Lily Salters. For goodness' sake, Mother, your memory has been somewhat muddy lately," he says, working his way toward the crust.

"Yes, of course, Lily," Roma says. "Anyway, while you were out doing god knows what with Lily…" She pauses and studies Thom. I never knew Roma had these interrogation skills. Maybe you develop them naturally when you become a mother. She continues: "We were talking. You know that Elwin's father—"

"Private," Thom interrupts, spitting a couple flecks of pizza crust.

"Don't talk with your mouth full. Yes, Private. Or whatever. He wants you to go on the river with your father and deliver his ashes. He said so in his will."

"I'm not sure *deliver* is the proper verb," Thom says, his mouth empty this time. "And technically, they aren't ashes. That's a misnomer. The cremains are mostly bone fragments, and they are ground up. Did you know the apparatus they cremate the body in is called a retort? Isn't that interesting? A retort."

"C'mon, Thom, a little respect for my father." I'm irritated at how lightly everyone is treating his death. It's my fault, I realize. I'm not wailing and gnashing my teeth. Maybe they are taking my lead. Still, it would be nice for somebody to feel sorry for me.

"See?" Thom says, delighted. "What you just said is a retort! Isn't that hilarious?"

Thom is giddy, like he's had a couple of beers and balances

on the edge of a decent buzz. I'm pretty sure soda is the only thing Marvin keeps in his machine in the back. Then it hits me.

"Are you high?" I ask Thom. It makes sense. The manic eating, the silly words that make him giggle. Maybe Lily was sharing more than a kiss. Maybe she dipped into her father's motel lobby stash.

"If you mean, have I taken a stimulant, then no, of course not," Thom says, looking me straight in the eye. "And no depressants either. But I do feel different, as if that last storm rolled through and changed me in the process." I'm sure Roma is dying to scream out, *Of course you're different. You kissed a girl for the first time. That changes things forever*, but I have to hand it to her—her lips remain sealed. "It's not like I've had an epiphany, but yes, Elwin, I am high on whatever this new sensation is."

Roma whispers under her breath, "Oh for fuck's sake," but Thom hears it.

"Mother?" he says. "What in the world?"

Roma plows ahead. "Before I was interrupted, I was saying that your father and I are worried about you getting in a boat again, I mean, after your last adventure. And by the way, we haven't had a discussion about that. That was pretty stupid of you."

"That is probably all of the discussion that subject requires, Mother," Thom says, reaching for another slice of pizza.

"I think what she is trying to say is, are you okay with getting back on the river?" I ask. "I'll be with you."

"So will I," Roma says, glancing at me. We have not settled that issue yet, and here goes Roma, throwing it out there like a done deal. I don't feel up to an argument.

"If we can all fit in the boat safely, yes, we'll all go," I say.

"Can Lily go too?" Thom asks, his eyes suddenly wide and bright.

"C'mon, Thom," Roma says.

"What? She would love to go. She enjoys adventure. So does Willie Nelson," he says. "He might like to return to his origins." Willie Nelson snoozes on the edge of the bed. One of his ears twitches when he hears his name.

"Honestly, I don't want any of you coming with me," I say. The three of them—Roma, Thom, and Willie Nelson—glare at me like I'm their prison guard. "What I mean is, I can't imagine it's going to be a fun time. We're spreading someone's ashes—my father's ashes."

"Not really ashes," Thom singsongs.

"You be quiet," I say, and the sudden shift in tone sends a dark wave across Thom's eyes. "That's not important. Not one of you has said a thing to try and make me feel better about my father dying. It doesn't matter how he and I felt about each other or how long it's been since I talked to him. He's gone. A human who was here a couple of days ago is gone, disappeared. And it hurts me in places that none of you even know about. So, yes, we are going on the river. Thom, you are going with me. The cat is not going. Roma, if you can sit in the boat and not bounce around, you are going. You can't drink any coffee before you come. Thom, your new little girlfriend is not going with us. She's not family." I'm out of breath when I finish talking. I've never spoken to either of them this way, because I've never been around them long enough to get this worked up. We're all seeing different sides of each other. Maybe that's the reason we're here, together.

Thom throws his half-eaten slice at the box and stands up. "She is NOT my girlfriend," he says. "You retract that." But before I can say, *Now, that, son, is a retort*, he sprints to the door and swings it open. It crashes against the wall, and Thom runs into the parking lot, Willie Nelson an orange streak close behind. I want to be upset, but a grin creeps across my face. The kid who knows the ins and outs of cremation, who sometimes acts like he's a middle-aged college professor, just turned back into a thirteen-year-old right in front of our eyes.

He's still a kid. Now and then he needs to be reminded of that.

29

Well, hey there," Linda says, swinging her front door wide. "Actually, both my hips is doing fine." A bright-eyed smile spreads across her face, and she nods slightly toward my waist. I realize I'm holding the Old Man's shiny, fake joint in front of me, like a church offering plate.

"Sorry," I say, dropping the prosthetic to my side. "I brought this because I thought you might know somebody with a drill press." We're in the process of confusing each other.

"Let's start over," I say. "Good morning, Linda. How are you doing? Looks like the rain has stopped, doesn't it?" That's not a lie. The sun is burning off the mugginess from yesterday's storm.

"Well, good morning. Would you like some coffee?" The mention of coffee makes me remember Roma and the way she's been swilling motel-brand packets of dark roast. My stomach does a little flip.

"I'm good," I say, and Linda pushes the screen door open, motioning me inside. She's wearing orange, puffy bedroom slippers that are two sizes too big for her.

"You probably didn't even recognize your old house when you drove by."

She's right. The house where I grew up has been painted a different color—now it's a cheery blue instead of dingy white. The couple that bought it from the Old Man added a garage, right over the spot where I wore the grass to bare dirt, pounding it with a basketball all hours of the day and into the night. The hill in the front yard that I used to think was massive is no more than a tiny slope, as if the weight of the years has worn it down. The few pines that remain there are so much taller, spindly and limbless until maybe twenty or thirty feet up, and the hedge the Old Man planted on one of his unusual and unexpected weekends home has grown thick enough and tall enough to block the view of the neighbors' back porch.

Linda's entry hall is lined with oil paintings of Lowcountry South Carolina scenes—lots of Spanish moss and dark-water rivers and crumbling tobacco barns. She catches me staring. "I'm in a painting group with some ladies from the church. Keeps our brains from turning to mush. My friends did these. They're better artists than me. Your father saved all his pictures of you boys. They're in a box in the basement. He said he didn't have the wall space at the river place, but between you and me, I believe it hurt him to see y'all's face on a regular basis," she says. I can't tell if Linda is trying to stir something up or just stating facts. She's one of those people who rarely worry about what comes out of their mouths. She reminds me of Thom.

"Have a seat," she says, leading me into a den. The small coffee table is covered with piles of neatly folded laundry. I smell dryer sheets in the air.

"I'm sorry," she says, scurrying to gather up the clothes. "I sort of forgot those were there." The clothes belong to a man—jeans and T-shirts and boxer shorts, the kinds of things the Old Man wore. "I always did your father's laundry. This load was in the dryer the morning I found him. I guess I'll take them to the poor box down at the church, unless you want them. I don't mean to upset you."

I want to tell her it's okay, but the words scramble in my mouth. There's a lot whirling around those piles of clothes: the fact that he'll never wear them again, the fact that my mother isn't the one folding them. You can't help what zips into your mind's eye. Memory has a way of intruding at the precise time it should keep its distance. Linda stops, waiting for me to say something, and when I don't, she disappears down the hallway, her arms full of clean clothes.

She's gone longer than it should take to set down a few stacks of laundry. Through a large bay window I can see into the back, and beyond that, across a vacant lot and into my old yard. I know it's impolite to leave where I've been placed and wander through the house of a person who, for all intents and purposes, is a stranger, but I feel myself drawn to Linda's backyard.

The grass has been recently cut, but it's still thick and lush under my shoes. Everywhere I look I spot low-growing color, flowers in pots or lining well-tended beds. Pink and white impatiens and some red vinca. Every bed is neatly mulched. A bird feeder swings from a low-hanging dogwood limb. I can tell Linda spends a lot of time and energy here. It looks like someone cares. I wander to the edge of her backyard and peer across, in the direction of the garage add-on.

Earlier, when I passed my old house on the street, I slowed and stared, but I didn't notice the post, the creosote telephone pole where my backboard and hoop used to hang. But there it is. The Old Man cut a square backboard out of three-quarter inch plywood and a two-by-four frame. He painted it white and he bolted it to the post, then levered the whole contraption into a hole he and I dug. We filled the hole with concrete mix and water. "Give me a lever long enough, and I'll move the world," he said. I was twelve. I had no idea what he was talking about. That evening I shot basketball until I could barely see the new white nylon net draped from the hoop. Once a bat followed my shot through the sky, diving away from the ball and the backboard at the last second. I suppose I'm lucky that couple left it up, like a bare signpost for my past. The backboard and hoop have long ago fallen away. Maybe it was too much trouble to dig the pole out of the concrete. I can't remember the last time I thought about basketball and bats and my backyard.

"Why did you bring that with you anyway?" Linda startles me. I didn't hear her walk through the grass.

I'd forgotten I'm still carrying the fake hip joint in my hand. In fact, I've got a death grip on it, squeezing it like somebody's going to attempt to steal it out of my palm.

"I came by to ask you a couple of things. First off, I was wondering if you would like to be there for some of the baggies and ashes thing."

Linda knows nothing about the ashes excursion. I never had the chance to fill her in at the funeral home, so I quickly run through the story—about the will, about starting at Baker's Bridge, about the bends and dumping the ashes when we round them, about the Old Man wanting Thom there. I tell her I plan to go that afternoon and ask if she'd like to be at the bridge when we leave.

"I don't think there's going to be enough room to fit you in the boat, but I thought you might like to see us off," I say.

Linda wants to think about it. "Not sure I'm up for that," she says. "I'm not family." She waves her hand like she's dismissing that subject.

"Second thing," I say, "I need to put some holes in this hip joint. Where in town could I find somebody with a drill press? You can drill into titanium, right?"

"Drill holes?" she says. "What in the world for?"

I don't want to get into explanations. "Just a couple of holes, for something I need to do."

"Well, I figured it was for something. I'm the curious sort," she says. "My cousin Skeet has a bunch of big tools. I can give you the address. He could probably do it. He's real handy. I'll call him and tell him you're on the way." She stares at her shoe tops. "Listen, I appreciate you asking me to come with you to the bridge. You know, your father and I…" She pauses, measuring what she is about to say. "People didn't understand. You didn't understand. But the two of us, we understood it all real well, and that's what has mattered during these years. I hope you can see that now. You know, come to think of it, I'd love to be at the bridge when y'all take off."

Her phone rings loudly inside the house. I'm not used to people with landlines. "I should probably get that. Let me know what time y'all will be at Baker's. You can get to your truck around the side of the house." She fast-walks toward the ringing phone, then calls over her shoulder. "You ought to see if that couple over yonder will let you walk inside your old house. They're nice folks."

The strip of thick woods that used to run behind all our houses and separate us from the railroad tracks is gone. In its place, a new row of houses—small, boxy ones built even closer to the tracks. I wonder how those people sleep at night, then I recall how many midnights I spent waiting for the sound of the whistle to come, like an alarm telling me it was safe to close my eyes. I don't know if it's the recollection of the train whistle splitting the night or a final glance at the lonely creosote post, but I begin to cry again. Not sobbing—my chest doesn't heave. Tears crawl down my face, and I don't know why. I don't miss this neighborhood. I'm not sad because a hundred feet away is the house where my mother got sick and withered away. I'm not crying because there's a window on the far corner, a window in my old room where I watched Lonnie Tisdale's mother run to our front porch one evening, looking for her lost boy, already sensing the worst the world could strike her with. Because mothers do that—they feel things early. I never came down the stairs, never told his mother the things I knew.

I wonder if the Old Man predicted I'd come by here, that I'd see the creosote post (the post he must have stared at a thousand times from Linda's perfect little garden), that I'd hear the memory of a train whistle. When I pull out of Linda's driveway and head for Skeet and his drill press, my eyes are dry, and I don't so much as glance at the little hill and my old house, and I don't stop and ask for a tour.

I've got no need to see how the past has been renovated.

30

Linda wants to see us off at Baker's Bridge *and* greet us when we arrive at the Old Man's place. I'm worried this is becoming too much of an event. I'm not sure the Old Man wanted the to-do—me and Thom and Roma ready to crowd into the boat, Willie Nelson roaming the dashboard of the Mercury, Linda on the bank, her hand on Lily's shoulder, so she won't walk toward the shore. Maybe he knew it would happen this way. Hell, he's predicted most of this, so far.

Earlier that morning, after I left Linda's house, I ran by her cousin's shop and explained where I wanted the holes drilled in the hip joint. Skeet was nice enough. He didn't ask many questions around the plug of tobacco jammed in his cheek. All he did was raise his eyebrows and repeat, "Well, okay then" over and over. He said I could wait while he drilled the holes, but I had to pick up the jon boat at the shack. I said I'd be back. "Well, okay then," he told me.

The jon boat was right where Ruby and I had left it, down the hill near the dock. I dumped the rainwater from yesterday's storm and loaded it in the pickup. I don't know why I glanced into the window of the shack, but when I did, my eyes locked right on the red ceramic chicken on top of the fridge. I'd forgotten about that bird. According to the will, it belonged to Linda now. The last time I'd been in the shack—when I was going through the Old Man's stuff—I hadn't even noticed that chicken. It would have to stay this time. I didn't want to deal with somebody's ceramic bird when I had ashes to spread. Plenty of time to tell Linda about it later.

And now, here we are, this odd collection of people left behind in the Old Man's wake. Lily grips her paperback of *Great Expectations* like it's trying to escape. I think she's probably upset that she can't go in the boat, but there isn't enough room, even as tiny as she is. Plus, on the way out of the lobby door at The All Excellent Inn, Marvin said, "I don't want that girl near the river. She ain't exactly water familiar."

It's called Baker's Bridge because the parking lot where we're standing used to belong to Baker's Furniture. The store loomed on the bluff over the river, on the last bend on what was then the outskirts of town. Everything has changed now, expanded, evolved, whatever. Baker's Furniture is long gone, and a new building sits in its place, a squat brick doc-in-a-box that appears to be hurting for business, judging from the empty parking spaces. But the bridge is still there, same as ever, the thick cement pillars slicing the current that runs high today because of the weather that's been blowing through.

"Y'all going to have enough room to float under there?" Linda says. She's got a point. We're starting on the upriver side, where below the parking lot a gentle slope leads into the dark water. On the downriver side of the bridge, there's nothing but kudzu and slick clay—no way to launch a boat in there. Between the underside of the bridge and today's water level, there's probably a good six or eight feet of clearance.

"We'll be fine," I say. Linda's question puts Thom on edge; I can see that. Roma isn't looking too confident either. "I've done this before. I've been here lots of times."

I knew Lonnie Tisdale would show up when I got to the bridge. No way to avoid it, I suppose. The last time I stood in this parking lot, I was thirteen years old, and Lonnie Tisdale was still missing. My father brought me here to watch the sheriff's deputies drag the river bottom with their hooks, looking for the last of Lonnie. My mother didn't want me watching them drag the river. Before we left the house, she said, "He's only thirteen," and the Old Man told her, "That's exactly why I'm taking him." He thought it was time to teach me about death or letting go or not placing blame on yourself. It didn't take. A salesman inside Baker's Furniture saw Lonnie jump and didn't think twice about it. Lots of boys jumped off that bridge, especially in the summer. But the water was too low that day. If he'd jumped after a rainstorm, like today, the world would have stayed the same. He knew better, but Lonnie Tisdale jumped when he shouldn't have, into low, bad water, and everything changed.

I stare at the river flowing faster than usual and imagine what that black water covers up. How much has gone beneath the surface and never come back? Or finally floated up, changed forever? The thing about a river is, it's always different and it never changes, both at the same time. I've missed this river and I hate this river and I can't wait to put my feet in it and I hope it runs dry. It's a mystery and it's a solution. It's everything and nothing. It took Lonnie Tisdale away, and it put me on the road only a few years later. Goddamn river.

I stare into the water until Thom says, "Elwin, we have cremains to deliver," and that brings me back to the world where people stand in a parking lot, holding baggies stuffed with a dead man's ashes. That's the real world.

The three of us—Thom, Roma, and me—walk to the water's edge, where the boat waits. I'm not sure what I'm supposed to do. This is the first location the Old Man wanted the ashes spread or released or expressed or whatever the correct term is for opening a baggie and dumping what's left of him into Black River. I stand in the wet sand, baggie #1 in my hand.

"Should you let them go off the bridge, up there?" Roma asks. "I mean, he mentioned the bridge by name, right?"

I don't have the time or energy to tell Roma why I can't walk up on that bridge and look down into the water. The water is so high, it wouldn't be a scary view, but I'd still see Lonnie Tisdale or maybe what he struck, lurking there, just under the surface.

"Am I supposed to say something at every place? Like a eulogy? I didn't think about that," I say.

"Elwin, an update. The boat seems to be moving," Thom says, panic creeping into his voice. The current has begun tugging at the bow of the jon boat where he sits.

"God, what is it with that kid and boats escaping?" Roma says and grabs the handle at the stern, then eases the boat back onto the sand. She rearranges the three life jackets on the seats. Simultaneously, Roma and I notice Thom gazing up the bank at Lily, like an explorer about to leave his woman and set out for new territories. Roma rolls her eyes and catches me watching her. She smiles, because we both know why Thom can't take his eyes off Lily Salters. It's a strange, satisfying feeling to share a secret with someone. I wonder if we'll ever tell Thom what we saw around the corner of The All Excellent Inn as the storm rolled in.

I take off my shoes (blue New Balance, size eleven and a half) and wade a couple of steps into the water, but everything begins to feel a bit too Biblical, so I back out until my toes are just at the edge of the current. I open the baggie and hold it away from me, like I'm expecting the insides to smell bad, and before I turn it over, I make a quick check of the breeze. I don't want the Old Man blowing back on me.

"What should I say?" I repeat, not realizing Linda can hear me up on the bluff.

"Just tell him goodbye," she calls down. I'm beginning to like Linda even more. She doesn't hesitate to cut to the quick.

I turn the bag over, and the ashes fall in a heavy cloud into the dark water, settling on top like a thin gray island. The ashes take a second or two to react with the current, but soon they drift downstream, and when they depart, my mind's eye is suddenly populated with faces. I see the Old Man, the way he looked the day of Lonnie Tisdale's funeral, when he brought me to the river and let me wash the grief off my skin, when he told me not to drift off, to stay where he could see me. I see my mother and her tired smile after working a long, late shift at the hospital. I see Lonnie Tisdale—how happy he was the day he rode his bike to my house to show me his brand-new fake eyeball. They are all together, floating in my head, drifting like ashes on a rain-swollen current.

"Climb in," I say, motioning to Roma.

"I'll see y'all at the river house," Linda yells down. "We'll be waiting."

31

On Thom's last river expedition, he was probably too busy splashing and hugging the hull of that Black River boat to notice the silence on the water. It's new to Roma as well. They both comment on it when we're out of earshot of the traffic on the bridge.

"It's usually even more quiet," I say, "but with this high water, you hear more gurgling and stuff." I find myself wanting to tell them every detail I notice as we drift along. How high the water is on the cypress trees. How we won't see any sand bars because of the rain. I didn't think about that when we took off. I'm sure the Old Man envisioned us stopping at the white bends between Baker's Bridge and his shack, pulling the boat out onto nice wide strips of beach and conducting our little baggie ceremonies. He couldn't have planned on the storms and the rain and the high water. Even the Old Man couldn't foresee the weather.

A quarter mile in, the shallowest of banks have disappeared. The river creeps right over them, right into the swamp. I've been on this river before after hard rains. I know what happens, especially farther downstream, where the channel narrows.

"This looks like a bend to me, Elwin," Thom calls out from the front of the jon boat, and he's right. We've reached the first place after the bridge where the river turns back on itself. Like I'd figured, no beach appears on either side of the channel.

"Are we supposed to do this while we're moving? Just dump them out?" Roma says, assuming I have a plan. She should know better.

I dig my paddle against the current and guide the boat toward the cypress at what I think is the edge of the swamp. "Tie us off on one of those knees," I say to Thom, and he instantly panics.

"Knees! Knees! There are knees?!"

"The stumpy things," I say, forgetting no one's told him cypress trees have clumps of knees jutting out of the water. "Loop the rope over. You can do it." I back-paddle and fight the current to keep the boat from drifting out of reach of the cypress.

Thom lassos one of the knees, and the boat pulls tight against the rope. "I did it, Elwin!" he yells out. "I kneed us. I'll have to tell Lily about this. I wish I still had my notebook to record things such as this."

Roma rolls her eyes again, a smile beneath them. The current swings my end of the jon boat into the cypress knees with a gentle, metallic bump. A large dead-fall limb lies crosswise among them, which seems to me a good place to tie the back of the boat, so we won't waver in the current while we deal with the baggie.

The familiarity returns—the tug of the current in the direction of the coast, the sound of a paddle slicking through the water, the birds screaming deep in the swamp. I used to spend hours drifting and fishing and forgetting all the things I'd left on the bank. Lonnie Tisdale and I did just about everything you could do on Black River. One day at Gilland Park we even pulled a kid out who was drowning, that addled boy William Bundrick. I don't think I ever told Thom about that. He would give it a new number. Sure, we'd done just about everything on the river. Lonnie was the only one I know who died on it.

The one thing I have forgotten is to pay attention to my hands. The Old Man taught me a long time ago that your eyes go first, then it's your hands' turn. "Don't go reaching into places you haven't checked out first with your eyes," he said more than once. "If you get a chance, poke around first, too, with a stick." Growing up, I knew people who didn't look or poke before they reached. Some of them ended up on the wrong end of a water moccasin. And though we are in the shank of summer, when almost every bushy overhang has a cottonmouth twirled around a branch, sunning itself, waiting to drop into a passing boat, I haven't thought about it since we set off from the bridge.

So, when Roma screams and points, it's too damn late. I've forgotten to look before I reach, and a cottonmouth the size of a kid's arm swirled on the thick dead branch already has me lined up, like he's saying, *Just a couple more inches and you are in my space, friend, and I do not tolerate people in my space.* He launches his strike as I jerk my hand back, but we both know I'm screwed. The strike catches me on the end of my index finger, and he latches on. I feel one of the fangs dig in behind my fingernail, and the bastard won't let go. I manage to shake him off but rip a slice in the tip of my finger for the trouble.

I have never liked snakes, but I've never been afraid of them. I always thought we had a healthy respect between us, so I've never imagined what it would feel like to be bitten by one. You might think there'd be this immediate panic and fear. Or perhaps a sudden flash into the future, where you see yourself sick and dying, your flesh turning dark and useless. But none of that happens. I just watch the snake sliding toward the far bank, his big head high in the water, his body carving figure eights through the current, and while I watch I think, *Well, he was just protecting his limb from some giant idiot. This is my fault. I ought to look before I reach.* I don't think about getting sick or dying or any of that. I'm thinking how stupid I was in front of my son. Maybe he'll learn from it.

Roma, on the other hand, goes crazy for all of us. She sees the shredded end of my pointer finger dripping blood into the boat and picks up her scream right where she left it a few seconds earlier. The jon boat rocks when she bounces up and down on her seat.

"What just happened?" Thom yells, and I realize he didn't see any of it—the snake or the bite. He was facing away from the trouble. He turns and catches sight of my finger, and his eyes widen. I see him trying to connect the dots. Maybe he thinks Roma did something to me.

"Elwin, that is a great deal of blood for one finger," Thom says.

He's right. It is a lot. It doesn't help that I'm shaking my finger up and down, slinging blood into the bottom of the boat, and I guess that goes with being bitten by a snake: you start doing additional stupid things. Shaking my finger isn't going to help anything. The fact that one of the fangs laid the tip of my finger wide open might be positive; blood coursing the wrong direction—out of the body—may carry some of the venom with it. But my finger is already beginning to swell, and I decide I'm in trouble. I wrap my bloody finger in the shirttail of my T-shirt and twist it snug, then put my hand between my legs, hoping nothing will flow north, toward my heart.

"What are we supposed to do?" Roma says. She's stopped screaming, and the sudden quiet is almost as bad.

"I don't think I can paddle," I say. "I probably shouldn't." Paddling will make my heart work harder, pump more blood. I need to slow things down. "You just have to steer the boat. The current will carry us. I don't feel all that bad. My finger hurts, but only a little." I unwrap my T-shirt to have a look, and the finger is growing bigger by the second, now the size of a cheap cigar.

"I can't steer a boat!" Roma yells. "Why do you think I can steer a boat? Jesus!"

"I'll do it," Thom says. He's already spinning in his seat to face us. "It shouldn't be that hard. It's basically physics. Do I need to be in the back of the boat to steer? Yes, I guess that would make sense." He starts to climb toward Roma, and when she slides to his right, the boat nearly tips.

"Hey!" I scream, and the two of them freeze like kids caught stealing cookies. "Everybody stop moving." I tell Roma how to shift to the front between Thom's legs, and he moves to the center bench. Then the two of us swap, and Thom grabs the paddle. I show him how to put his hand on the top and the other halfway down the shaft. Roma unties us from the cypress knees. The current snags the front end of the boat and pulls it downstream.

"Hold on," I say without realizing how stupid that is. There is no way to stop at this point. We are moving, and Thom is figuring out that when he strokes on the left, the boat goes right. Like he said, physics. "Roma," I say, and when she turns, I toss her a baggie.

Without me having to say a word, she opens it up and empties it over the side of the jon boat in the direction of the cypress knees. The ashes settle into the water and mingle like powdered creamer in black coffee. Among all the cypress knees, the current becomes confused and backs up on itself, so the Old Man's remains drift in several directions at once. The water is shallow enough, I see a few curious redbreast hovering below the cloud of ashes, wondering if it's some sort of fish food. At least I think I'm seeing this. My head is becoming a little light.

"Head for the house," I say to Thom.

"Cheating death again," Thom says back, and I hope he's right.

32

Thom keeps the jon boat more or less in the middle of the river. If I had the time, I'd be proud of him. He shouldn't have to worry about strainers with the water this high. We'll float right by them.

Good, I'm still thinking clearly. Every couple of minutes I tell Thom to correct his steering left or right, but I must say, he's doing a nice job. And he's sweating. I don't think I've ever seen my son sweat. I'm sweating too, but I'm not paddling a boat. My head is drenched, and I feel as though I'm sitting in a sauna. Roma and Thom notice it, I can tell. But they don't want to say anything. A couple of times, Roma asks if there's anything she can do, but when the answer is always no, she understands and stops.

We pass a bend. I nod at Roma, and she pours a baggie of the Old Man's ashes into the river while we're moving, and when she does, she starts crying a little, but I think the tears might be more for me than the Old Man. She's scared. We all are.

We flow along, the same speed as the cloud of ashes on the surface of the water, and I wonder if Lonnie Tisdale is down there somewhere. I can't look long, because my balance is starting to go, and the weight of my head wants to pull me into the water. We are having to do all of this on the fly. There's no stopping now, no ceremony. The Old Man will have to understand. Roma suggests that I could come back some other time and finish up with the baggies, which is a good sign—she thinks I'm going to be alive tomorrow. But I have no intention of doing this more than once.

I just want to close my eyes. The way the river tugs us is making me a little sick, and if I close my eyes, I won't have to watch the water flow.

"Maybe you shouldn't do that," Roma says, poking me on the thigh. "You ought to stay awake. That's what it says here." I'd forgotten that Roma has her phone. She's googled something, probably *What To Do When You're Delivering Cremains and Get Struck By a Water Moccasin.* "It also says you might have a minty taste in your mouth. Do you have a minty taste in your mouth?"

I didn't, until she said that. Now, my mouth feels like it's full of wintergreen Lifesavers.

"What's your skin look like?" Roma says, staring at her phone. "It says it might start getting discolored. Should I call an ambulance? Where should I tell them to go?"

I don't want to look. The next time I see my fingertip, I want to be with somebody who knows what to do about the damage. Roma has distracted me, so I'm not keeping up with Thom and his paddling. I don't know where to tell an ambulance to go. The Old Man's place? We might not make it there.

"Uh, Elwin," Thom says, and I hear the frantic sound of him paddling backward, fighting the current. I glance at him, and he's pointing downstream, and the look on his face is more confusion than fear. Ahead of us, the river narrows and veers into the stands of thick-trunked cypress. In normal water it would be easy to follow the thin channel. In fact, there would probably be sandy beaches on either shore. In low water you might even have to get out and drag the boat across a couple of places. This is different. All the extra flow from the rain heading downstream has turned this section into something of a lake. The obvious river channel has disappeared, and ahead it looks like nothing but cypress and still water. We drift quietly into the trees, and the quiet blankets us.

"Where am I supposed to go?" Thom whispers, his paddle out of the water.

"Do you feel any current?"

"I did just a second ago," he says, louder. "Now it's disappeared, Elwin. I don't feel anything." We glide slowly among the trunks, and I look for any sign of the river channel. I've heard about this. The Old Man used to scare me with stories about guys who got turned around in the swamp, either in a boat or on foot. Sometimes they didn't turn up for days. I can see why. Every direction mimics every other. I can't tell where we've just been, much less which way to go. I don't like losing my way.

My finger is still wrapped tight, but my hand begins to swell, like I'm wearing a puffy winter glove. A vague memory of this part of the river flickers into my head, and I try to recall how far we have to go until the shack. "How many baggies do you have left?"

Roma looks between her feet. "Three," she says.

So we're pretty close, I think. The leftover cloud cover from the storm and the new thickness of the cypress have made it hard to see the sun. I am hoping to get some sense of direction, figure out where east and south are, but when I tip my head, the tops of the cypress swirl into a kaleidoscope of leaves and needles. "Stop us from moving," I tell Thom. "But be careful where you put your hands. You don't want to get bit by a snake." I laugh at that, but the two of them don't join in.

Thom bumps the front of the jon boat into the trunk of a huge, old-growth cypress, and Roma half-hugs it after she checks for anything that might be wrapped around the back side. The tree is too big to put a rope on, so the side of the boat sort of anchors there, spinning in a lazy circle, not so much from the current but from Roma squirming in the front seat.

"We need to be heading south," I say. "I know that."

"Well, that helps a lot," Roma says. She has recovered from seeing a snake attached to my finger. Her old tone is returning, and in a strange way, that makes me feel better. I feel the skin stretching on the meat of my hand, but I won't unwrap my finger. I don't want to see what I have to deal with.

"Mom has a compass on her phone," Thom says, his voice climbing a ridge of excitement.

"I do not," Roma says.

"It's an app."

She says, "I have never put a compass app on my phone," and Thom explains to her that the compass app is there whether you want it or not, and their voices fade and turn tinny, as if they are arguing in the bottom of a barrel. I can't keep two thoughts balanced in my head, so I realize that I am losing the ability to reason and make decisions. I shake my head to clear the fog that's forming and almost fall out of the boat. Roma grabs me by my waistband and tugs me back onto the middle of the seat.

"We have to keep moving," she says. "And maybe you ought to put on that life jacket." Thom starts in about the compass app again.

My head clears a bit, and I remember one way to find the current is to look for bubbles below the surface and see which direction they flow. Bubbles head toward the coast too. I lean over the edge of the boat, Roma still with a fistful of my pants, and there, just beneath the surface of the cola-colored water, I spot a tiny trail of clear bubbles moving the way we just came, or where I *guess* we just came. I don't want to take my eyes off them in case they switch direction. I'm about to tell Thom and Roma that we don't need a compass, that we can just follow bubbles, which shouldn't be hard, shouldn't be difficult, even for a rookie paddler like Thom. And I'm about to say all these things, lining up the words in my mouth, because I'm beginning to feel like the words themselves are bubbles, and when I open my mouth they'll more than likely release into the air and float in the direction we're supposed to paddle. Suddenly, though, just inches below the surface of the water, right where I'm staring, Lonnie Tisdale shows up, his head angled so his good eye stares right back at me. He still has that summer haircut, the short buzz he got a few days before his last jump. And Lonnie Tisdale is grinning his toothy grin, probably because he thinks I'm going to die on this river, so he won't be the only one of us who accomplished that feat. I want to tell Lonnie Tisdale that he's wrong, because the sheriff's deputies won't have to drag the river for me. I'll be delivered to the bank in a jon boat by my son, ferried to the dock in a floating hearse, my son's mother perched over the bow like a figurehead on a sailing ship, pointing the way.

Lonnie Tisdale's face floats even closer to the surface, bringing the rest of his body with him. I see the jeans and long-sleeved shirt he wore when he jumped. That's when everybody knew he'd taken that second jump on purpose, because he dressed for it. Nobody in Kingstree wore jeans and long-sleeved shirts to the river in summertime. A scream builds in my throat, behind the word-bubbles. There are things that want to escape from my mouth, thoughts boiling up to the surface that have been buried so long, they don't know how to act. It took a snake to bring them to the surface. A snake and Lonnie Tisdale. Lonnie told me what he was going to do that day, what he was thinking of doing, told me not to repeat it. He told me he got so sad sometimes that all he could think about was jumping off Baker's Bridge and staying under the water forever. "That will show them," Lonnie said. "They'll think about me then."

He said he jumped the first time for fun and lost an eye. He said he would jump again and show them. "I won't be sad anymore," he said. "Don't tell anyone I'm going to jump," he said. "Don't you breathe a word." I was thirteen years old. What are you supposed to do with that kind of confession when you're thirteen?

"Why would you tell me something like that, Lonnie?" I say. Roma and Thom stop arguing about the compass app and stare at me. I don't realize I'm crying until Roma says, "Is it the pain?"

You can't be a confessor when you're thirteen. Lonnie Tisdale didn't know that. Neither did I. All those years, I kept Lonnie's promise. I never told anyone I knew about the darkness that rose in Lonnie's head. I knew he might jump. I didn't tell his momma. I didn't say a word when she came to our door that evening, looking for her boy. I could have given her some peace.

Lonnie Tisdale jumped because he knew what was under the water, and now he lives there, and if anybody can tell us which way the river runs, it's Lonnie Tisdale. I rub tears out of my eyes with the T-shirt on my swollen hand and see both of Lonnie's arms stretch out like he's pointing two directions at once, and he has that smile still stitched on his face. I haven't seen that smile in fifty years, the same one he had that time he showed Laurice Reeves his fake eyeball and kissed her on the mouth under her porch light, the same smile he flashed across our dining room table all those nights when he stayed for dinner at my house. Lonnie Tisdale's head bobs a bit in the water, which means there's a current coming from somewhere. His head wouldn't move without a current.

"Lonnie," I say, pushing back the scream and releasing a string of word-bubbles. "We can't go in two directions. You're just messing with me."

Maybe I do scream a little, because behind me Roma says, "What the hell are you yelling about?" I don't look away from the water because I don't want to lose sight of Lonnie Tisdale.

"I think he's going into shock," Thom says, which doesn't surprise me. Thom seems to know everything.

"My boy is smarter than you and me ever were," I say to the water, hoping the word-bubbles break the surface and reach Lonnie Tisdale's ears. It occurs to me that Lonnie Tisdale may not recognize me. He still looks thirteen. I wonder what I look like to him.

Roma pulls on my shoulder, and I slap my wrapped-up hand on the gunwale to keep my balance, but putting it down means I let go of the T-shirt. My finger is out in the open now. The pain knifes up my arm and erupts from the top of my head. That's when a scream blows out of my mouth, but I don't take my eyes off Lonnie Tisdale, and I think he appreciates that. He drops one of his arms to his side and points with the other to the left, into the trees, a direction I would have never considered going. Then his body wiggles in that direction, and he swims off like a slow, lazy fish.

"He wants us to follow him," I say and point to the left with my swollen, flayed finger. When I don't feel the boat move, I finally tear my gaze away from the water, toward Roma and Thom. They stare at me, their eyes wide and wondering.

"You're soaking wet," Roma says.

"A snake bit me," I say, still pointing, thinking that explains everything. "Lonnie Tisdale wants us to go left, into those trees. That's south. Just follow Lonnie. He knows." I dip my head low again, close to the water, but all I see is darkness. No faces, no arms. "That way," I say, and I feel the stroke of Thom's paddle, and we follow the thin trail of faint bubbles Lonnie Tisdale leaves in his wake. I hope Lonnie forgives me. I hope everybody does.

33

I don't believe in ghosts. Then again, I didn't believe I'd ever be bitten by a snake. Belief becomes as worthless as dirt when a cottonmouth latches on to your index finger and his poison works its way up the freeway of your veins or arteries. I can't remember which way those flow, those veins and arteries, which carries and which returns. We follow Lonnie Tisdale, because it's the only option available in the swamp, because Roma can't figure out how to find the compass app that Thom swears is on her phone. They are too tired or scared to argue anymore, scared because I'm seeing ghost-bodies in the water that lead us south through the cypress.

My finger is out and pointing, sticky from the blood, but honestly, I can't tell you if I have my eyes open or shut. The one time I know I'm truly looking at something, I focus on the finger. Even though it's swollen, it has a withered appearance, turning a nasty shade of red and purple. The filleted skin on the tip is brown at the ragged edges where the single fang ripped a path from the very end to the first knuckle. I raise it in front of my face for a closer look, and Roma says, "You should probably cover that up," but she doesn't believe what she's saying. Like I said, snakebites tend to warp belief. I don't re-wrap the finger, but I do stick it out, in the direction of due south, in the direction of Lonnie Tisdale.

When Thom and Roma talk, which seems to be constantly—as if they are trying to ward off fear and misdirection with a stream of words—the sounds come to me from far away. The two of them are in another county and not just another seat in the same boat. Thom is becoming decent with the paddle. When Lonnie Tisdale bubbles to the surface and tells me to change direction, Thom easily follows my finger. When Lonnie reappears, I want to tell him I'm sorry, tell him that for years I've smoldered with guilt because I didn't tell anyone about his dark thoughts and his darker plans. But he disappears before I can make the words come together in my mouth.

Roma says, "Is this a channel? I guess it could be. We could be just going farther into the swamp. Do you think we're just going farther into the swamp? We're following a guy who's pointing with a finger that was in a snake's mouth. He doesn't know which way is which." She thinks I can't hear, but I don't have the energy to fight with her. Thom knows. He's following the finger. It strikes me as funny that when people run low on options, they'll follow the first one you offer up. I don't care. I'm following Lonnie Tisdale. He knows this river. He lives here.

Above their talking—literally above all of us—I hear a brushing in the air, and it takes me a second to recognize the sound of wind in the uppermost branches of the cypress. The temperature is dipping, I think, but I don't trust temperature right now. I'm still draining sweat off my forehead. Then, in the distance, a low drumroll of thunder drones in the treetops.

"That's not good," Thom says.

"Paddle faster," Roma says. Everything that comes out of her mouth now carries a ring of desperation.

"I can't paddle any faster in these trees," Thom says. He, on the other hand, is pretty calm. I'm very proud of him. I should tell him so, but my tongue has grown thick in my mouth, as though it belongs to someone else. I'm not even sure I can form words. "I'm relatively new at this, Mother," Thom says.

I'm sad that they've forgotten about me. At least it feels that way. I want to be important to them, so I keep pointing. Lonnie Tisdale leads us down a U-shaped path, and it feels like we've completely reversed course on a watery switchback. A flash of lightning lands on our right, back in the swamp, and before the sky recovers, a crack of thunder blasts through the trees. The storm is right on top of us, resting on the crowns of the cypress.

"Do you think that was a bend?" Roma says, but without waiting for an answer, she unceremoniously dumps a baggie of ashes into the water, and because she is in the front of the boat, the cloud of gray cremains floats right by me, masking Lonnie Tisdale's face. That's why I scream.

"What?!" Roma screams back. She thinks we've run up on another snake. She doesn't know that the Old Man's ground up bone fragments have obscured Lonnie Tisdale. I could tell her exactly why I yelled if my tongue weren't the size of a bar of soap. Roma wags her head from side to side, looking for the newest snake, because she knows that in the front, she'll hit it first. She doesn't notice that the channel we've been following suddenly widens, and quietly, without fanfare, we're out of the cypress and into deeper, faster water. We don't need Lonnie Tisdale anymore, not at the moment. That's why he disappears. Not because he was ducking the Old Man's ashes, but because he was finished pointing the way. He did not mention the storm before he left.

When the channel opens up, there's room for wind, which steamrolls across the surface, dragging sheets of rain with it. I want to tell Roma, *That's funny, isn't it, how the rain started all full bore and everything? It didn't work itself into a torrent. It just started at full speed. Isn't that strange?* I wonder if this is always the case—that the more you can't talk, the more interesting things you have to say.

The drops, fat and fast, bullet the surface of the river, churning it. I stick my finger straight up in the air, like I'm pointing toward God, but what I'm really doing is washing the poison away. For some reason, I think that rainwater will make everything better. Roma and Thom don't see it that way. Thom pulls hard on the paddle, and he looks like a man with a job to do. *My son looks like a man.* I like the way that sounds in my head. Roma covers her face with her hands, and I guess she is crying. With the wind and rain that arrive in noisy waves through the air, I can't hear what is happening behind her hands. I want to tell her, *That's funny, too, isn't it, how if you cry in a thunderstorm, nobody can really tell?* Again, interesting things pop into your head when your tongue is too thick in your mouth to say a word.

"Put your finger down," Thom hollers at me, and he has a point. I should probably keep it below my heart. It's always best to keep things below your heart. That's pretty good. I should put that on a bumper sticker. Maybe on a T-shirt. If I participated in that social media stuff, I would put it out there for the world to see. Everybody in the world has a heart. I already miss Lonnie Tisdale.

"Look!" Thom says, and this time he is the one pointing. He has only one hand on the paddle. *Don't drop the paddle, son.*

Ahead of us, camouflaged by the shrouds of rain, is a dock, and above the dock, on a tiny bluff, is the Old Man's little house. I spot the outline of the Mercury beside the shack. The car's headlights are on, and someone leans on the horn in short bursts. Again. And again. And again. I realize *that* is what I've been hearing in the background since the storm began—someone in a squeaky Mercury Cougar sending out a signal, the car perched like a lighthouse on the bluff.

I slump on my seat, my hand below my heart, and before I shut my eyes, I see Roma empty a baggie over the side, and the raindrops pelt the Old Man until he disappears, and I think, *Well, we goddamn did what he asked. We brought him home.* That's when my body gets very heavy.

34

I have never put much stock in secondhand information. Its accuracy depends on who's attached to that second hand. But I have to go with it this time, because in this case, firsthand information is pretty sketchy, which sounds funny, because my hand—my *first hand*, I guess—was the size of catcher's mitt by the time Thom steered the jon boat to the Old Man's dock.

I recall little snippets of what happened after I felt the boat bump the dock, tiny photo-flashes of faces and driving rain and an orange cat behind a front windshield and my son hugging Lily Salters. I remember that clearly because Thom has never appreciated anyone touching him, unless he knows about it in advance and can plan for it. He couldn't have planned for Lily grabbing him around the neck—that's about as high as that tiny girl can reach—and pulling him close in the sheets of rain. *A movie scene*, I think, when it flickers into my brain later.

I don't recall much about Roma and Linda, but I know they were there when we hit the dock. Linda had a small umbrella, I think, but it wasn't doing much of a job keeping her dry, the way the rain drove horizontally off the river. The rest is pretty much a blur. Like I said, faces and water and hugs.

The secondhand info truly begins in a hospital room. Thom sits in a chair in front of me. I have no idea where Roma is. I have no idea where I am. To my right, the sun streams through a window with no blinds, and beyond the glass the sky is a cartoony blue. The last time I saw the sky, it was filled with lightning and thunder and water.

"So that's what we have in common, Elwin," Thom says, and I realize he's just finished a train of thought I haven't been following. I've been busy wondering how the sky got so blue.

"Sorry," I say, "I missed some of that."

Thom sighs. "To recap, you cheated death just like me, Elwin," he says. "The doctor told us because of the way the snake bit you and where the snake bit you, you could have died. But you didn't."

Roma walks in carrying a large plastic cup. "Here," she says and hands it to Thom. "Don't drink it too fast." She looks toward me and rolls her eyes. "It's Coke," she says, and I know why her eyes are spinning. She read somewhere that kids on the proverbial spectrum should avoid caffeine, so Thom had been serving a lifetime ban from soda. Now he's sucking Coke through a straw like a man who's been thirsty for years. Things changed while I was asleep.

"Can you bring me up to date?" I ask Roma, and she pulls up a second chair.

"How far back?"

"From the dock. I remember the rain at the dock, then things get extremely fuzzy," I say. "Oh, I remember Thom hugging Lily. That's part is clear." Thom smiles behind the straw in his mouth. He's not even embarrassed.

"You don't remember us leading you up the hill? Anyway, Thom and I helped you up the hill, and Linda tried to keep the rain off you, which didn't make a whole lot of sense, since we were all soaking wet anyway."

Thom takes a break from the straw. "You kept saying, 'Below the heart, below the heart,' then you would proceed to stick your hand between your legs. Extremely odd behavior."

"You were saying a lot of things." A hint of a smile breaks across Roma's face. "We got you in the car, but when we opened the door, Willie Nelson made a break for it."

"I sort of remember that," I say.

"He's fine now," Thom says. "We went back for him the next day, when the rain had quit. He was waiting for us. He was not pleased, but he's recovering, emotionally."

"We got you to the hospital fast. Linda was mad we hadn't

called an ambulance or called her. We told her we weren't thinking too clearly. We told the doctor in the ER what bit you and how long ago it was, and here we are." Roma waves her arm like she's revealing a prize on a game show, and that's when I notice the IV pole next to my bed, a tube running into my arm. A few inches below the IV needle the gauze wrapping begins. The size of a cantaloupe, the wrapping covers every bit of my wrist and hand.

"It was an adventure," Roma says. "And that's pretty much it."

"You cried a lot," Thom says, pulling his straw from the drink and pointing it at Roma. "You couldn't stop, Mother. Elwin and I cheated death, but you pretty much cried during the entire episode."

"I don't think that's important," Roma says. She shoots Thom a withering glare.

"That's not all," Thom says. "There's an addendum."

Roma rises from her chair—too quickly it seems. My brain is beginning to clear. "The doctor said he would be back in a few minutes. I think they are going to discharge you later on today. Maybe tomorrow. Then you can go home. We can all go home. I'm tired of that hotel—"

"Motel," Thom says.

"Whatever," Roma fires back. She's talking fast, like she needs to fill the air with words before the conversation jumps the tracks. "I can drive Thom back if you need to stay longer, but we haven't really talked about that because of what's been going on. We should make some plans. Plans are good." She's speaking so rapidly my brain starts to fuzz up again. Tiny, clear drops flow down the tube into my arm, and I think about Lonnie Tisdale and the bubbles in the water. I want to ask them about Lonnie Tisdale, ask if maybe they saw him too, but I decide it's better to keep my mouth shut.

"You're avoiding it," Thom says, again waving his straw pointer.

"Avoiding what?" I say. "Did something else happen? Is Linda okay?"

I'm not sure why, but I think Linda might have been involved in some sort of lightning-and-umbrella incident.

"What? Linda's fine," Roma said. "Jesus, Elwin, can you just talk to the doctor?" I don't know Roma well enough to recognize when she's dodging something. She tilts her head at Thom and hardens her eyes, the universal signal for *shut your mouth.* Thom has never been good with the signals people exchange.

"It's your finger," Thom says.

I glance down at the huge ball of gauze on the end of my arm. Somewhere under all of that wrapping, my snakebit finger waits.

"For god's sake, Thom," Roma says. "You just can't button it up, can you?"

"My inability to shut up isn't exactly breaking news, Mother," Thom says, and he has a point.

"What?" I say.

"Your finger," Roma says. She's given up waiting on the doctor.

"The snake finger," Thom says.

I try to lift the gauze, but it feels like a bowling ball sits inside the wrapping.

Roma takes a lingering breath. "They had to take your finger," she says. "They had to amputate. I mean, they kept asking me if I could make that decision for you, and I kept telling them to wait until you were awake, but the doctor was afraid to wait. Something about your finger already being septic. He said it was the best thing."

"You lost a finger, Elwin," Thom says. "But you cheated death. All in all, you came out on the positive side of the ledger."

I try to wiggle my index finger inside the big ball of gauze, but I can't tell what's moving and what's not, what's missing and what's not.

"I'm sorry," Roma says. "I wanted the doctor to tell you.

He's probably more used to relaying that kind of information. It's a mystery to me."

"You have nine other good fingers," Thom says. "You're still opposable, sort of. You're still human."

It's like they want to keep talking—in their special ways—to prevent me from saying something. Or maybe it's to keep any awkward silence from crashing into the hospital room. But honestly, I don't know what to tell them. I stare out the window at the blue, blue sky, and I'm thinking about how I didn't die from a stupid-ass snake biting me on the tip of my finger, and Thom's right, that's probably a fair trade—a life in exchange for a couple of joints of finger material.

It could be worse. It can always be worse.

35

I leave the hospital the next day, a finger short of two full hands. The doctor is a thin, perspiring man with an accent from somewhere far, far north of here. More than once he throws the phrase, *You're probably wondering how I ended up in Kingstree*, into our conversations. I never wonder that. I'm more concerned with my finger, which I don't see (or see the space it used to occupy) until the morning they release me. I ask the sweaty doctor if I can look at it, and his face suggests that's the most idiotic question in the world. I tell him, "I want to be around a professional when I see it for the first time." There isn't much of a wrapping on it now, just some gauze and some white tape.

My missing index finger is the perfect definition of the word *nub.* I believe the person who invented that word had less than ten fingers. I am expecting the whole finger to be gone, but the northern doctor took it off at the knuckle, so I still possess the ability to point, with half the previous effectiveness.

"The stitches will have to come out in a couple of weeks," he says, "and we can get you some occupational therapy, you know, to help you adjust." He re-wraps the finger carefully, with less gauze than before, and tells me how important it is to keep it dry for several days and how important it is to take the antibiotics he gave me. "That was one seriously infected finger. How big was that snake? You don't get many snakebite cases where I'm from," and he's dying for me to ask him where, exactly, that place is. I don't bite on it. I don't care. He took my finger, so I don't owe him a thing.

Linda picks me up in the Cougar. Her wide car eats up every inch of space in the lane reserved for patients leaving the hospital. I'm waiting in a wheelchair when she pulls up.

"Are you okay?" she says, then, "a whole wheelchair for a lost finger?" You always know where you stand with Linda. I wonder if that's what the Old Man eventually latched on to—someone who asks the quiet questions out loud.

The slow-walking orderly who wheeled me down says, "You take care of yourself now," and I point my wrapped-up half-finger at him and shake it a little, and his eyes widen.

"Oh, that will take some getting used to," Linda says and shuts the door on me.

Roma and Thom are waiting for us at the motel. Linda says, "You mighta guessed, they'd have some sort of surprise cooked up." In fact, that hasn't crossed my mind, and I make a note that Linda, for all her good qualities, is probably not someone to trust with your secrets.

At room 113, I see a bright yellow banner strung above the entrance that reads *Welcome!* Roma and Marvin sit in lawn chairs flanking the open door. When we pull up, Roma turns and yells into the room, and quickly, Thom and Lily fill the space. I know these festivities are only due to the missing finger. If there had been no snake and no fang and no Lonnie Tisdale just below the surface of Black River, there would be no welcoming party. Instead, they would have been mad about getting soaked and lost in the cypress, and for all I know, Roma and Thom would have already hit the road for home. Funny, I had to lose a couple inches of finger to get a party.

Before Linda cuts the engine, she says, "Oh, I almost forgot." She reaches into the back seat and grabs a wrinkled plastic bag. "My cousin finished drilling this thing for you. He said to tell you he won't charge you. He said it didn't really take that long, plus you lost a finger. I think he felt sorry for you." She hands me the bag. "Sorry, I peeked. I still don't get it."

I'd forgotten about the Old Man's fake hip joint. It feels strange, digging around in a plastic bag for something a doctor *added* to a body, when a doctor removed something from mine a couple of days ago. Life can turn ironic without much effort, which doesn't seem fair.

"That was nice of him," I say. "There's not much to get, really. Just something I need to do."

Marvin is high as a pine. He can't take his eyes off the wrapped-up finger when we step out of the car. "You want to see it?" I say, and Marvin leaps from his lawn chair.

"The hell," he says. "I'll throw up if I see something wrong on somebody. I always been that way. If I see somebody in the grocery store missing an arm or something, I switch aisles." I want to ask Marvin if he encounters a lot of amputees in the Food Lion. There are things I don't know about this town, I suppose.

"We thought you might like a little celebration," Roma says.

"Lily and I have been reading up on snakebites," Thom says. "We have concluded that you were very fortunate." Maybe that's what serves as a date for these two: soaking up internet information about venomous snakes in the Southeastern United States. Maybe Lily lays a kiss on him between articles. I sort of hope so.

"I have to catch you up on some things too," Roma says. "Let me get you a chair."

It feels good to sit. I'm a little disappointed Thom doesn't want to join us in the shade of the awning outside our rooms, but I guess we've reached that point—where the adults and the teenagers create their private conversations, a demilitarized zone of silence between them. I thank Linda for the ride before she wheels the big Mercury out of the lot. I hate to see her go. Linda has become somebody to depend on.

Willie Nelson slinks out of 113 and weaves between my bare legs. I'm wearing the same shorts I had on in the jon boat, but I'm pretty sure they've been washed. *Linda again,* I think. He arches to sniff the end of my wrapped finger but pulls back quickly when he catches a whiff that doesn't agree with him. I wonder if he senses something I should worry about. I've heard cats can do that.

"I'd pretty much given up on that cat after he ran off in the rain," Roma says. "But it was like he was waiting for us when

Thom made us drive back to the river. I spent the whole ride wondering what I was going to say to him about death and animals and stuff. But Willie Nelson was there. Not even muddy or hungry or anything."

"Cats are a source of surprise most times," Marvin says, and he suddenly sounds like a news broadcaster, his voice dipping low and sincere. He glances around like we're being watched, then reaches into his shirt pocket. He pulls out a joint the size of a ChapStick tube and hands it to me. "Something for your rehab. Call it a sleep aid. Call it what you will." He slides it into my hand, the one with all the fingers. I smell the stickiness of the weed from a couple of feet away. I bet I'll sleep like a baby.

"Jesus, Marvin," Roma says. "There are kids inside."

"Kids know more than we realize," Marvin says. I haven't spent enough time around Marvin to know if he always talks in poster-worthy proclamations. But I kind of like it. I wonder what he sounds like when he's not stoned.

Marvin heads down the breezeway, and Willie Nelson considers following, but remembers who feeds him and retreats into the room. Thom must have said something funny or clever because Lily giggles behind me.

"I'm so sorry about your finger," Roma says. "You think it's something you'll get used to?"

"Oh yeah," I say. "All things considered, it could've been worse."

"Listen," she says. "I feel like I sort of let you down," and I think she's going to mention the way she cried during the thunderstorm and didn't really help get us out of the cypress. I should know better than to predict where Roma is headed.

"Okay, I was supposed to empty all those baggies out on the way down the river, but I guess in the trees and the thunder and lightning, I missed a bend or didn't notice in the rain and all that. But I ended up with an extra baggie. What I'm saying is, we still have some of your father's ashes, and I'm not sure where they are supposed to go. I'm sorry."

I suddenly feel the difference in our ages. Roma sounds like a teenager confessing a bad deed to her father. A wave of exhaustion washes over me, and I settle deeper into the chair. It's funny how little we know each other. She doesn't realize that the last place I wanted to be that afternoon was on a river, sifting ashes into the water. The only reason we were there was that I didn't want the Old Man haunting me the rest of my life. She's waiting on me to say something, to absolve her in some way, so I can't tell her that I don't give a shit. At this point, somebody could wash the rest of the Old Man down the toilet in room 113, and I'd be fine with it. I feel myself getting mad about missing a finger. Something else has been taken from me, and it all has to do with that river and the Old Man and Lonnie Tisdale. The past settles on my shoulders and pushes me even deeper into the lawn chair.

"Look," I say, and Roma's eyes are trained on me, waiting. "You got nothing to worry about. I don't really care that much about it, to tell the truth. It's not that important, considering everything else." I wave my missing finger in the air for emphasis. Roma's eyes turn a little hard.

"Well, of course it's important," she says, probably louder than she intended. The mumbling in the room behind us ceases, as if Thom and Lily have switched to eavesdropping mode. "That's the last remaining part of your father, and he wanted to end up in that river. You have to go back."

"I don't *have* to do anything," I say. "He's dead. He'll never know."

"Yeah, but you will," and she nails the whole idea of haunting. It's not about ghosts or goblins showing up in the night. It's about the things that live in dark folds of your brain, the memories and obligations and broken promises that nag you forever, like itches you can't possibly scratch. She's right, of course. If I don't do something with that baggie, I'll never be able to shake it out of my head. Maybe she knows me better than I realize.

"There's something else," she says, and I hear new embarrassment in her voice, a sound she rarely makes. "In all the excitement and whatever—you know, with the thunder and rain and your snakebite—well, there was a lot going on at the dock when we got there."

She's right. All those images of what was happening when we found our way out of the trees and made it to the Old Man's dock are fuzzy and continuously evaporating. What I remember most is a lot of water, dropping from the black sky, flowing past the banks.

"Yeah?"

"Well, anyway, we were mostly concerned with getting you up the hill and getting out of the storm." Roma pauses. I can tell she's avoiding the best part of the story. Or the worst part. "So, you see," Roma continues, "nobody thought to tie up the boat to anything on the dock. It kinda disappeared."

Kinda disappeared. That strikes me as funny. I'm not sure anything can *kinda* disappear. It's either gone or not. Then again, the Old Man has *kinda* disappeared. A bag full of him still exists. The Old Man's dock is cursed; boats tend to magically float away from it.

"I'm really sorry," Roma says. "I suppose that boat was yours, technically. I apologize for losing your boat. Maybe it will turn up somewhere."

I want to tell Roma that if somebody runs across a solitary jon boat, the first thing they are going to do is scrape the license decal off the side and go fishing in it. That crooked boat is long gone, but I don't care. It wasn't mine long enough to miss. Plus, it's become the snakebite boat. Bad juju inside that aluminum. I won't mourn its *kinda* disappearing.

"Again, not a big deal, Roma," I say. I want to make her feel better. That's a new one for me. Seems like a lot of new things are happening. Maybe that's what I should expect, the more I hang around people I don't know all that well.

"And there's something else," Roma says.

"Jesus, Roma," I say, "how much more you got?" It's not that I'm irritated. I'm just done with hearing about things I've missed out on. It's tiring.

"This is the last one. You know that Ruby woman, the funeral person? She won't let up about you selling that river property. She thinks we're married or something. She came by the hospital once, and let me tell you, she wasn't just visiting. She was hanging around like a vulture or something, seeing if you were going to die. So I told her you were fine, and she starts firing away with her sales pitch. I don't like her."

"She says I can make a lot of money." I thought about that while I was lying in the hospital—how I could sell that property and be done with it and escape with enough money to quit worrying at the end of every month. I mean, I'm not poor, but I'm a long, long way from rich. I'd like to be happy somewhere between the two.

"Oh," Roma says. "I thought you didn't want to sell. I was kind of mean to her. I thought I was sticking up for you. I guess I was wrong." I've never had anybody stick up for me. It's a strange new sensation. Roma had my back.

"I don't know what I want, Roma," I say. "I just lost a finger. I need some time." I wonder how long I'll be able to use a missing finger as an excuse. "I appreciate you, though."

Roma's eyes soften again, and as if she detected an invisible signal in the air, Ruby Floyd wheels into the parking lot and comes to a crunchy halt in front of us.

36

Ruby Floyd is not pleased to see Roma sitting in one of the lawn chairs. She grimaces through her window. Beside me Roma tenses, scrunching down in her seat, making herself smaller. Roma was not exaggerating, I suppose, when she told me she and Ruby weren't all that nice to each other. They obviously haven't let it go yet. Some people have a hard time putting a dull edge on their grudges.

"Rumor has it I almost had you for a customer," Ruby Floyd says as she unfolds from her rusting Bronco. She ignores Roma. I believe Ruby's talking about the river property and her being my real estate agent; then she nods in the general direction of my missing finger. "But you're still alive and kicking."

Small towns are like that. The bad news and the good news get bounced from person to person like a pinball. Everyday life never gets talked about. But somebody loses a finger to a snake? That's top-shelf gossip.

"I'm just lighter by a couple of inches," I say, holding up the white wrapping. Thom comes to the door to see who's attached to the new voice.

"Those aren't really summertime shoes," he says, staring at Ruby Floyd's untied brogans.

She tips her Panama hat toward her feet. "I go with what's comfortable," she says, "and speaking of that, I want to talk to you about that river house again." I'm not sure what old shoes and comfort have to do with the Old Man's place. Ruby Floyd is not a master of segue. Or maybe she's the greatest of all time.

"Not now, please," I say. "It's been a long couple of days."

But Ruby isn't letting this chance evaporate. Again, she recites her warning about the horde of people moving upstream, a well-heeled tidal wave from Charleston, burdened by the weight of their money, and they need something into which they can sink their aforementioned heavy burdens. While she talks I concoct this ancient image of a string of camels ridden by Bedouins leaving the dusty desert of Charleston, searching for a new oasis.

"He hasn't decided anything," Roma says, leaping into the middle of Ruby's sales pitch. "He lost a finger, for god's sake. You people." Even Roma is using the missing finger as an excuse. The *you people* comment has a little spice on it. Ruby doesn't bat an eye.

"I have a couple coming to the funeral home today, and they want to look at river property. I'd like to show them yours," she says. "They are primed to buy. They are bringing their checkbook with them. These people will put a deposit down before you can blink."

"We're not blinking," Roma says.

Thom is confused. "You are selling Private's house?" he says.

"Who is Private?" Ruby says. Her eyebrows arch slightly, probably because she thinks there is *another* river property ripe for selling, owned by somebody named Private.

"Why did no one tell me about this?" Thom says.

"Private is none of your business. It's family," Roma says, glaring at Ruby.

I want to use this moment to explain to Thom the fine art of being quiet. He doesn't realize that if the two of us shut up, the next few minutes could be full of entertaining slings and arrows, if we simply let Roma and Ruby go at it themselves.

But suddenly everyone talks at once. Thom tries to explain to Ruby who Private is while Roma fires off at Ruby about how stupid it is to try and sell something that isn't for sale, and Ruby keeps droning on about the Charleston Bedouins with their trunks of money. I listen to it for a few seconds because, honestly, it's interesting to hear everybody waste their breath. Willie Nelson appears in the open door for a look, his head bobbing in the direction of one person, then another, as if he's watching a tennis match gone bad.

In the midst of it all, I hold up my wrapped nub, testing the air for wind direction. The crowd goes instantly silent. Even Thom. I never knew a missing digit could have such power. I should remember that.

The problem is, with a finger in the air and the sudden silence, they wait for something profound to emerge from my mouth. And I got nothing. We stare at one another for a few seconds.

"Elwin?" Roma says finally. "You were about to say?" My finger is still hoisted in the air.

The best I can come up with is, "I was about to say that I'm tired." The three of them are unimpressed, but I push on. "And, Ruby, I might be at the river place tomorrow morning. If you want to come by with the Bedouins, we'll be there." I wave my nub in the general direction of Thom and Roma, so she'll know what I mean by *we*.

"Bedouins? You mean the Hamptons," Ruby says. I forget I'm the only one aware of my desert wanderer analogy. "They are here today only and I don't—"

I point my missing finger at her, and she shuts up immediately. I'm beginning to like the power in my nub. I can make the world go quiet with one easy motion.

"Tomorrow, Ruby," I say. "I have other things to do today. Thom and I have a couple of errands to run."

"Errands?" Thom says. "Can Lily come?" I know the point he's reached—the one where the little girlfriend gets invited everywhere.

Before I answer him, Ruby slinks back to her Bronco, accepting her minor defeat. I know she won't leave it alone, though. Ruby isn't the type of person who tosses in the towel. She grinds the gearbox, hunting for reverse, and the squelch sends Willie Nelson scurrying inside.

"I don't like her," Roma says. "I think she has a crush on you."

"I didn't think old people had crushes," Thom says, again voicing what most people keep to themselves. He retreats into room 113. I haven't seen Lily in a few minutes. I wonder if she snuck out while the tornado of conversation was whirling.

"She has a crush on the Old Man's property," I say. "Got nothing to do with me."

"We'll see," Roma says. "I don't like her. She isn't good for you." Her eyes have changed again. This time I think I see a little jealousy leaking out of their corners.

This is a morning of so many new things.

Part IV

The Bridge

37

I don't plan on sleeping through the afternoon, but I'm still recovering, still flushing drugs and whatever else got into my system. A couple of times Willie Nelson jumps lightly onto the foot of the bed and curls in the crook of my bent knee, like an orange nurse checking my vitals.

From the slant of the sun behind the blinds, I know it's late when Roma knocks quietly on the door and tells me she and Thom are leaving early the next morning. "This whole vacation I'm supposed to be on is over," she says. "I need to get back to work." Then she adds, "some vacation," mad that she spent most of it in a little town with a dark river running through it. Or maybe she's annoyed that she enjoyed herself.

Technically, my visitation with Thom is over. Roma's Independence Celebration has run its course. Doesn't mean I can't be sad that the two of them are leaving me on my own again. A weekend every now and then is going to feel tame compared to runaway boats and poisonous snakes and powdery cremains.

"I told Thom we're hitting the road as early as we can get moving," she says. "He's not happy. All the blood drained from his face." Roma doesn't get it. Thom isn't simply mad; he's in love too. That pair of feelings often travels together. It hasn't crossed Thom's Lily-struck mind that room 113 was always a temporary situation, which means, of course, that Lily is temporary. Roma or I could manufacture some story, tell him that we'll all be back, that we'll let him come visit Lily. Or we could make up some kind of bullshit about how they can write to each other and stay in touch. But Thom is smart enough to see through that. The blood fleeing his face is the recognition that his first big crush is rushing toward a crashing halt. That always sucks the life out of you when you're thirteen.

Who knows why things click in your brain? It doesn't happen all that much in mine lately. Blame the residual painkillers in my bloodstream. Or blame the panic I feel when Roma says the Independence Celebration is over and she's leaving with our son the next morning, but I make a decision in that second. I know what I need to do before the sun sets, but we must go quickly, I think, glancing again at the remains of the afternoon seeping through the blinds.

Roma tells me she's not sure where Thom is. "He said something about having to go load the soda machine with Lily." There aren't enough customers at The All Excellent Inn to drink a soda machine dry in only a few days. *Loading the soda machine* has no doubt become their euphemism for making out.

"You don't think they'll get all desperate and do something, well, you know…" Roma says, edging toward the door. She wants to hunt for her son.

"Let's just wait," I say. I figure I can give him fifteen minutes before I go looking, but Thom is back in five, his eyes watery and red. It's the first time I've seen my son cry because of something he lost. Those are a different flavor of tears. I want to tell him the good news is that he won't have to cry like that often. But I know better than to talk about it. Roma does too. She has decent instincts at times.

"I need your help with something," I say to Thom, and there's no protest, which surprises me. I figured he'd want some wound-licking time. Roma doesn't mind that she's not included. She probably wants to squeeze in another hour of independence.

Thom doesn't ask to bring Lily, doesn't ask to let Willie Nelson ride in the truck. In fact, he's stone-silent for the first few minutes as we roll through town, then finally: "Where are you taking us, Elwin?"

"You'll see," I say. "It's no big secret." A couple of minutes later, I pull the pickup into the lot of the doc-in-a-box that sits on the hill above Baker's Bridge.

"Why are we back, Elwin?" Thom says. "I don't want to be here."

"Me either." I reach under the seat of the pickup and pull out the remaining baggie of the Old Man's ashes. They aren't really ashes anymore. During the storm, the top of the baggie must have come undone, and some rainwater or river water leaked inside. Now, instead of dusty cremains, it's more like clumps of mud that have begun to harden. The Old Man has some substance again.

"I'll wait here," Thom says quietly. *So this is where he wants to lick his wounds*, I think.

"No, you won't," I tell him and again, he doesn't protest. Any fight in him has vanished. "Come on." I nudge him toward the door.

Floating beneath Baker's Bridge in a boat has never bothered me, but this entire trip, I've avoided going to the top of it. I remember the last time I stood there. It was after Lonnie Tisdale made a stupid jump, the one that *didn't* kill him. It just took his eye. He started losing things a lot sooner than the rest of us. I look at my shortened finger. Only a small bandage covers the stitches.

Thom follows me down a narrow path that eventually rises toward the highway and the bridge. Baker's Bridge has probably been resurfaced, maybe even repaired, half a dozen times since I was last there. But like when I was a kid, there's no sidewalk, only a narrow strip of weedy shoulder, then the low metal rail. That's where all the brave or stupid boys climbed to dive off. The sun hovers above the tops of the cypress that line the river. It's been hot and dry in the days since I lost my finger, so the water is low and creeping below us. Thom notices the same thing.

"It wasn't that far down when we were here before," he says. "Things surely change fast."

That's the nature of rivers. There's always new water. The way the lowering sun strikes the surface throws odd shadows into the current. It's not hard to conjure up mysterious shapes, not hard to imagine the water as deeper than it really is. Lonnie Tisdale wasn't hoping for deep water that afternoon when he made his last jump. He didn't want anything to cushion his dive. I knew that before he went, and I kept my mouth shut. I wonder if the Old Man would think that was a show of strength. If I stare long enough, maybe I can spot what Lonnie Tisdale landed on. Maybe Lonnie Tisdale will stare back at me. Maybe after that last storm, he made his way against the current, upstream from the cypress swamp where he last showed his face.

I lose track of time, gazing into the black water, so I'm not sure how long Thom has been crying. He's not sobbing. Just small, breathy sniffles. He wipes his nose with the tail of his T-shirt.

"I'll be fine, son," I say. "You don't have to be upset about me." I want to tell him that I should have let Lonnie Tisdale go a long time ago, but I couldn't until I apologized to the face in the current. I want to tell him that his grandfather went out on his on terms, just him and the mosquitoes and the riverbank. I know how heavy death can weigh on a kid. I remember that feeling.

"Elwin, it is not anywhere close to fine," he says. "You don't understand."

"Of course I do," I say. "I've told you about Lonnie Tisdale and this bridge."

"I've heard all those stories. I forget the number," Thom says. "But this has nothing to do with you, Elwin. This is about me." His voice cracks somewhere high in his chest. He wipes his nose again. Though he's crying and his voice won't cooperate with him, he sounds older, as if he's gained a new layer of life in the past few days. "It hurts," he says. I recognize that look on his face. I'm an idiot. He isn't crying about me. He's crying for Lily Salters.

Thom is doing what we've all done. He thinks his pain is special, that nobody in the world has ever felt the way he feels right now. One day he'll realize that the dull ache he can't shake is as common as water. And that's not a bad thing. A sense of loss is a tie that binds us all together, no matter how precious we want our feelings to be.

"I know it hurts. It's like somebody has punched you in the gut and left their fist there, so they can twist it, just to make you remember. You've had a crush, Thom, and it's about to be over. You feel like you're going to die. You feel like you don't want to go through the day. You feel like you're never going to see that little girl again."

"Well, I certainly appreciate those words of encouragement. You're certainly not helping, Elwin," Thom says.

"Believe it or not, I am." I'm not planning what to say. It just flows out of me, like I'm one of those dolls that talks when you yank the string on its back. "The worst thing I could tell you is that everything's going to be okay. I could try to distract you or make you think about something else. I could tell you that tomorrow you're going to wake up and the world will be bright and happy and you'll laugh, and Lily will fade away like a puddle drying in the sun or something."

"That might help," Thom says. He leans forward against the metal rail on the bridge and braces himself with his arms.

"No, it wouldn't. It'd be a crock of shit, because you know what? You need to go through these things. You need to hurt. Pain gives you scar tissue, and scar tissue helps you get through the rest of your life. If me or your mom tells you everything is going to be okay and pulls down the shades on the real world, one day you're going to get the shit kicked out of you. I don't want the world kicking the shit out of you. Hold on to this feeling for a while. Live with it. Then pitch it out. Because it's done its duty."

I wish I'd been listening to myself. I wish someone had told me these sorts of things years ago. I could have let Lonnie Tisdale go. I've held on to him for so damn long.

Then, like a bolt of lightning coming from the absolutely clear sky, the story of Lonnie Tisdale's funeral flies into my head—#17, I think. I couldn't sit in the funeral, couldn't sit there in my baseball uniform with all my teammates—our little squad of honorary pallbearers—and listen to that preacher put Lonnie to rest. I had to get out. I remember throwing up just outside the sanctuary, and the Old Man leading me to the car and driving us out to his piece of land at the river. I never knew it existed until that day. None of us knew about it, not even my mother. It was the place where my father disappeared when the world got too big for him. *Kinda* disappeared.

I remember that afternoon—the Old Man telling me to take a swim, making me strip off my baseball uniform and get in the water. I remember lying back in the water and feeling the current tug at my legs, tugging me away from a funeral for a boy, away from the things that lurk under bridges and break necks, away from secrets you should have confessed. It wasn't a baptism so much as a good washing. The Old Man was trying to tell me the same things I'm saying to my son, but he wasn't a man of words. All he said was, get in the water. Don't float out of sight. He was trying to put scar tissue on me, and I didn't even realize it. I couldn't connect those watery dots back then. Now, a half century later, standing on the same bridge—maybe the same place—where Lonnie Tisdale jumped, I see what the Old Man meant to say.

"Elwin, what are you doing?" Thom asks. "Who in the world are *you* crying for?"

I forget about my wrapped-up finger and almost stab myself in the eye, dabbing at a tear. I could tell him, no one in particular. Or I could tell him I'm crying for Lonnie Tisdale's ghost or a dead father or women who are too young to be your wife or fingers that are gone or thirteen-year-old boys who've had their hearts stomped on. But that would be a lie.

"I'm crying because it feels good to let shit go," I say. I'm having trouble opening the baggie, what with my bandaged half-finger.

"Let me help you," Thom says. He parts the opening. The Old Man's remains resemble tiny pebbles of cement.

"Go ahead," I say. Thom pinches a corner of the bag and shakes the Old Man over the rail. I follow the gray clods in the air, and it seems as though they fall forever. I wonder if Lonnie Tisdale felt that when he jumped, that he would fall endlessly.

The bits and pieces of the Old Man strike the surface of Black River and part the current, the ripples quickly erased by the syrup-slow movement of the water. The clumps disappear almost as soon as they hit. I wait for Lonnie Tisdale to rise in the blackness below us, but he never shows his face.

Thom folds the baggie carefully and shoves it into the side pocket of his cargo shorts. "Am I going to feel better?" he says. The sun is about to dip below the cypress trees, yet there's enough light to see my son's face. He's stopped crying, but I see the hurt lingering behind his eyes.

"Yessir, one day. It'll just happen. It's magic, sort of," I say.

Thom steps away from the rail. "Just look at the two of us, Elwin," he says.

"Yeah, we're a pair, aren't we?" I say.

On the highway, maybe a quarter mile away, two pinpricks of light head in our direction in the lowering evening. Thom stares for a couple of seconds, then says, "Ford Taurus, one of the newer models." We edge near the rail to give the car plenty of room. I want to be safe. I'm not sure how visible we are on the shoulder of the road. The car slows when it catches sight of us and eases by. Thom's not even close. It's a fifteen-year-old Subaru.

"I guess my mind is on other things," Thom says. I put my arm around him, and he lets me. We take one last look from the height of the bridge, as if we are going to spot something fresh and undiscovered in the dark water.

That's the next to last time I think about Lonnie Tisdale.

38

The last time I think about him is the next day, long after Thom and Roma check out of room 115. While I stand there, watching Roma put their bags in her car, I sense she doesn't truly want to leave, and that plants a warm feeling in my stomach. She keeps rearranging how the bags sit in the trunk, as if they are filled with something fragile that requires tending. She glances at her watch a half dozen times, then at the sky. She peppers questions at me.

"Are you going to be all right?"

"How long are you going to stay?"

"Did you take your antibiotics?"

"How are you paying for this?"

"Are you sure you're all right?"

"I wish we could hang around a little longer, but you know we can't, right?"

I am beginning to see that Roma is a woman of many questions. She's not trying to be annoying or anything. She's simply the kind of person who navigates the world by interrogating it.

I don't have any answers for her. Maybe that makes *me* annoying, but it's the truth. I could leave today. I might leave tomorrow. I'm not sure how many loose ends I need to stitch together because of the Old Man and his passing. Death breeds paperwork.

"I need to think on that," I say. "This might take a while." I'm talking to Roma, but I have my eyes on Thom. He isn't saying much. He's buckled himself into the passenger seat. That dense, dull ball of pain still sits heavy in his stomach, I'm sure of it. Earlier, Roma asked him if he wanted to tell Lily goodbye again, and he shook his head. He is going to spend the entire trip home staring out the window, watching the trees race by on the side of the interstate, and he's going to relive every single moment he was around Lily. When he remembers that first kiss around the back corner of the motel, he'll reach up and touch his mouth. We've all been there.

Thom is so distracted pining away for Lily, he isn't much concerned with Willie Nelson, who perches in the window of room 113, watching the action through the glass.

"And you're going to keep the cat?" More questions. "You don't seem like a cat person. What makes you think you're a cat person?"

I figure I'm a perfect cat person. I care about as much for Willie Nelson as he cares for me, which is to say: not a whole lot. We can gravitate in each other's orbits as we see fit.

"Maybe Marvin can keep him," Roma says. "Sort of like a barn cat, but for a hotel."

"Motel," Thom says from the front seat. I didn't think he was keeping tabs on our conversation.

"I'm not going to pawn Willie Nelson off on Marvin," I say. "When I get home, if it doesn't work out, I'll think of something. Thom can come visit him at my place." I don't want Thom to lose everything that's wandered into his life the last few days.

"Lily wanted him, but her father wouldn't have it," Thom says. From my view through the back window, I see that releasing Lily's name into the air only adds to the weight on his shoulders. He shrugs lower in his seat.

"Call me when you get back to town," Roma says. "We'll get Thom a new phone as soon as we can. We'll try to keep his old number. You'll split the cost with me, right?"

"Of course," I say. I want to suggest that she see how long Thom can go without a phone, not because of the money, but because without a phone and without earbuds screwed into the sides of his head, Thom allowed new things into his world—real things, like Lily Salters and an orange cat.

I walk to the open window on the passenger side, and I see

what Thom's eyes have been trained on the last few minutes. Lily Salters watches him from the lobby window, the two of them spying on each other one final time. Her glasses glint a bit in the reflection.

"It's okay to feel terrible, you know," I say.

"I guess so, Elwin. I suppose that's how I know this is an important moment. If it didn't mean anything, I wouldn't feel this bad, right?" Thom says, and that's when I realize he is going to be all right. When you try to make sense of something that will *never* make sense, you're on your way back. "We cheated death, Elwin. We should be proud of that, agreed?" He reaches through the window and pats me on the arm, the kind of thing an eighty-year-old man would do. I'll probably never figure my son out, but I can live with that.

After Roma and Thom pull away, I grab the plastic bag with the Old Man's hip joint and open the driver's side door of the pickup. Like a trained lapdog, Willie Nelson leaps into the front seat and curls up in the morning sun. I swing by a True Value hardware I'd noticed last night when Thom and I returned from the bridge. I need a couple of long bolts, plus washers and nuts to fit them. Willie Nelson waits in the truck.

Willie Nelson knows we're getting near the river when we turn off the highway and hit the sand road to the Old Man's place. He rises slowly, stretches, then flattens himself onto the dashboard, scouting ahead for us.

I grab the little toolbox I keep behind the seat and think I might have a problem with a locked door, but the Old Man never believed in locks. The two of us—me and Willie Nelson—walk into the Old Man's house. I suppose I should quit calling it the Old Man's place. It's mine now.

Inside, the air hangs thick and musty. I prop open the windows. The screens are pretty much useless, a patchwork of frayed holes, but it's worth a few mosquitoes to air the place out.

"Dammit," I say out loud when I turn on the light and notice Linda's ceramic chicken on the top of the refrigerator. I've forgotten (again) to mention it to her. Losing a finger distracted me. I feel guilty for not following through on that one. The chicken sits so far back on the fridge, I need a chair to help me reach it. It's heavier than I imagined.

I'm not sure if I'm forbidden to see what's inside, but I know myself too well. There's no way I can give it to Linda without taking a look first. I pull the chicken head off and hold the body under the light. I don't even recognize what's filling the ceramic chicken until I grab a handful of the tiny scraps of paper. Ticket stubs, the customer halves. All of them from movies. There must be hundreds and hundreds of them. Some are your basic garden variety, generic admit-one paper stubs. Most of them, however, have the names of the movies printed on them. The Old Man and Linda saw everything that came out, it seems. Movies I wouldn't expect. *Beetlejuice, The Lost Boys, Candy Man, Heartbreak Ridge, Lord of the Rings.* I spot a couple of the *Fast and Furious* stubs. Horror films, dramas, romantic comedies. They drove to Lake City and Florence and Sumter. I reach deeper into the chicken and feel something solid. It's a roll of cash wrapped with a thick rubber band, mostly twenties and fifties. Under the rubber band is a note from the Old Man. It says, *This should buy you a few movie tickets. Keep watching, honey.*

When I stop crying, I bury the roll of cash again beneath the ticket-stub confetti inside the chicken and put its head back on. I don't know if I'll tell Linda I looked inside. She probably won't care one way or the other. I place the chicken on the floorboard of the pickup—so I won't forget it again—grab the plastic bag and the tools and head down the short bluff to the dock.

The water is still dropping, and the current gurgles against the posts beneath the boardwalk. Slow-moving shadows of a few bream or redbreast cruise the shallow water. A couple of them are the size of my hand. I should grab a rod and try to catch one or two for dinner, and that thought surprises me. I'm considering what's next, like dinner. I should be more focused on checking out of The All Excellent Inn and getting on the road.

When I took the Old Man's hip joint to Linda's cousin, he said he'd figure out how far apart to put the holes, said he had a dock cleat somewhere in his shop he could use as a template. I had to trust him on that. On the floating part of the dock, it takes me a couple of minutes to find the old holes in the gray, flaking wood, but there they are, the place where the previous cleat was anchored until a few days ago, when it pulled free and sent Thom downriver. The measurement between the holes is perfect, and the bolts I bought at True Value slide easily through the fake hip joint and into the holes in the dock. The plank is nice and solid. I reach over the edge and into the water. One of the edge boards on the dock has pulled out of its screws. It's all but coming loose. I'll have to bring some new deck screws and a new one-by-six and replace it. I'm working by feel beneath the dock with my left hand, but I thread a nut onto the bolt and hand-tighten it. I bought some extras because I figured I'd drop one or two into the river, and I wasn't wrong. But I've got plenty to cover my mistakes, and I tighten them down with a wrench, again working blind with my off hand. I'm going to have to get used to doing things left-handed. Missing a pointer finger puts you at a disadvantage.

It doesn't look exactly like a cleat, I think, but it fits tight against the dock, and with that silver ball sticking up in the air, there's something strong to tie off on. I admit, I was growing tired of things floating away from this dock. A wooden fishing boat, a jon boat, my son. The new hip cleat shines in the sun. It will be too hot to touch after a while. The Old Man would be happy that a piece of him will keep things tied up snug and secure. I reach into the plastic bag again. I had the old guy at True Value cut me a length of nylon rope, ten feet or so. I tie one end around the ball of the titanium joint and coil the bulk of it on the dock. Now, if somebody drifts up, they will have a way to keep from floating downstream. The bright cleat and the rope look too new for the dock. Somebody should replace these boards, I think. *Somebody.*

I don't know if the Old Man would consider his fake hip joint a ghost of his former self, but if it is, he's got a decent, calm view of the river in both directions. That titanium will last a damn long time, longer than the dock. He'll be able to see forever.

39

I don't hear the clank and rumble of Ruby's Bronco in front of the shack. When I walk up from the dock, sweating from working on the new cleat, she stands on the porch with a happy, perspiring couple that looks to be in their thirties. They obviously followed Ruby to the river; their fancy SUV is parked just behind the Bronco. Ruby spruces up a little for clients, I see. She has on a flowery skirt, and the brogans have been replaced with dark, flat pumps. Sensible shoes that look too new. I miss her unlaced boots.

She lies right off the bat. "Well, hello! What a surprise! I didn't know you'd be out here," she says. She's brought Mr. and Mrs. SUV out to the river to dangle the Old Man's property in front of their noses like a fat, watery carrot on a short stick. "These are the folks I told you about, the Hamptons—Colston and Mary-Frazier."

I've met plenty of women in the South who possess that odd double-name thing. Lots of Anna-Adeles and Mary-Burtons and Miller-Brookses. But I've never met a Colston. Sounds like a beer brand. He strides forward, his hand out. "Thank you for letting us take a look," he says, but I'm not ready to shake a hand with only four fingers on mine, so I leave him hanging. I can tell Ruby has reported that I'm a reluctant seller. They are putting on a full court press.

"This air," Mary-Frazier says. "It's so different from Charleston air. This air is so much fresher. I simply love this air. Don't you love this air, Colston?" Ruby's smile is plastered the width of her face, but her eyes are asking me not to say anything that might spin the conversation in a darker direction.

I'm still not sure I believe in ghosts. I don't know if the hip-cleat down at the dock will conjure up the Old Man and house his spirit there, where he can watch the river run. But as I stand there, watching old Colston and Mary-Frazier rock back and forth on their well-shod feet, waiting on me to say something gracious and welcoming, I feel the Old Man seep into my bones. He possesses me. I sense my shoes sinking into the sand and dirt where he walked hundreds of thousands of steps, and it's like I've thrown out an anchor. I feel the Old Man's words spill out of my mouth.

"Y'all don't sweat much for rich folks," I say.

Ruby's smile quivers on her face. Colston and Mary-Frazier don't know whether to laugh or beat a retreat. I won't let them off the hook either way.

"Did Ruby tell you my father died just a few days ago? Did she tell you about my finger?" I hold up the missing digit. The bandage is dirty and brown now. It suggests infection. "Did she mention the whole thing with the snake?"

"Snake?" Mary-Frazier says, as if she's heard a foreign word that needs translating. "Colston?"

Her husband is unfazed. He's dealt with people like me and the Old Man before. "Well, of course, they have snakes, sweetie. We're essentially in swamp land," he says, recapturing his smile. "Snakes are excellent swimmers," he adds, then grimaces at his misstep.

"They *swim*?!" Mary-Frazier shrieks. "Snakes can swim?!" She is imagining battalions of wriggling snakes making their amphibious landing on the shores of her new property. She glances down the bluff toward the water.

Ruby throws out a cliché of a life preserver. "Mary-Frazier, trust me, snakes are more scared of us then we are of them."

Colston ignores them both. He is here for business, and he's not leaving without a piece of river property to build his newest retreat. He nods at me. "I wonder if just us fellas might take a walk," he says.

Panic sneaks into Ruby's eyes, and her smile twitches. She doesn't like the idea that she's losing control of a client. I knew she should have worn the brogans. They would have made her taller and more intimidating. But she's also smart. She knows she shouldn't protest.

"Of course," she says, her voice striking the pitch of false cheeriness. "Mary-Frazier and I will have a seat on the porch. Watch the water run by."

A mosquito lands on Mary-Frazier's broad, bright forehead, just below her blond hairline. She hasn't felt it, and I should probably warn her, but maybe I'm doing her a favor by staying silent. She needs to know that there are things like snakes and mosquitoes at the river. You learn to live with the bites, even if one of them takes a finger from you. Behind her, Willie Nelson's head pops up in the window, and when Mary-Frazier turns, she catches sight of him. "Oh goodness," she says, "I'm allergic to cats. We can't possibly go inside. Snakes and cats… my lord."

"Sure," I say, ignoring her. "We can chat." I drop the plastic bag where I stand, the extra nuts and washers clinking inside it. "Let's go to the dock."

Down the path to the river, Colston carefully picks his way, trying to keep his shoes clean. He's wearing loafers without socks, around a size nine. The leather is soft, probably Italian. He might be limping a little. Probably a football injury at one of those fancy high schools in the state. Or soccer. He's more the soccer type. I feel sorry for him for a couple of seconds, but I'm over it by the time we hit the dock.

"Listen, Elwin," he says. I feel a slight twinge of violation that he knows my first name. The sound of it makes me think of Thom and Roma, working their way north, toward home. I hope Thom is feeling better, that the metallic ache in his stomach is beginning to lighten. I'm not doing what Colston requested—I'm not listening—so when I snap back, I catch him in mid-sentence. "…and we've always talked about it. You know, have a getaway, but not *too* far away, if you know what I mean."

I do not know what he means. There are certain kinds of people in the world who constantly construct escape plans and places to live them out. And all they really want, it seems, is more camouflage draped over their lives, something thick and broad to cover up all the shit that's wrong where they truly live. But maybe that's just me. I'm not familiar with the escape routes money provides.

"We've been in contact with Ruby for almost a year. Property on the river doesn't pop up all that often. You folks hold on to things, brother," he says.

You folks. Like we're an exotic breed of human. But that isn't what bothers me. It's the whole *brother* thing. Colston is one of *those folks*, the kind who call complete strangers brother, as if we're going to eventually hug or sip bourbon together.

Colston takes a breath. "MF is right," he says. "The air is different here. That air is worth something. How much do you want for your air, Elwin?"

Well, I think, *that didn't take long.*

Not a whole lot of chitchat. Right to point. I'll bet Colston weighed his strategies on the walk to the dock, trying to decide if he should chat me up for a while or dive for the bottom line right away. I wonder what I did to convince him which way to go?

"My father bought this place back in the early, early '70s," I say, and I watch Colston's shoulders sag a bit. He wants me to negotiate, not tell stories. He takes another breath, this time more of a sigh of resignation. He's going to have to listen to me.

"I've never really looked at the title, so I don't know the exact date. Probably not long after he got back from Vietnam. You've heard of Vietnam, right, Colston?" I probably shouldn't say that. It's a little mean-spirited, but I'm starting to care less and less about people I'll never see again. Colston is one of those. Even if we are brothers.

"We didn't even know about this place until I was thirteen or so. This is where he came to watch the river run and think and not have to worry about the world out there on the highway. I always thought it was because of what happened in Vietnam, with his stomach and all. Did Ruby tell you about my old man's stomach?"

Colston scans around for a place to sit. He's afraid this is going to be a long conversation. The muffled voices of Ruby and Mary-Frazier drift down the bluff toward us. Somebody—I can't tell who—is laughing too loudly.

"No matter," I say. "Long story short, all he could eat was really soft food, like mashed potatoes and casseroles, for the rest of his life. I found out about this place—we all found out about it—one day when he brought me down here. It was about this time of year, now that I think of it. After a funeral for a friend. My friend, I mean. He brought me here because he thought I needed the same thing. He thought I needed to watch the water and to think. I was thirteen."

"What happened to your friend?" Colston says, about to miss the point of the story. A full-on sweat has popped out on his forehead, which makes me think about Mary-Frazier's brow. I wonder if that mosquito got what he came for.

"He jumped off a bridge and he drowned," I say, "but that's not important. What's important is that the Old Man knew I needed the river. He knew it was the only thing that could help me."

"Is that a hip joint?" Colston says suddenly, pointing to the edge of the dock. "I'm an orthopedic surgeon. That's a hip joint. What is a hip joint doing here? You can't use a hip joint for a boat cleat." He walks toward the edge of the dock for a closer look. "You know, all implants have a serial number, so you can tell who it belonged to and when it was implanted. How long has this been here?" he says, bending over the cleat. It shines like a beacon in the sun.

I don't remember that loose board until I hear it begin to give way with a dull crack. I should have warned him about it, I suppose. Colston performs a tight pirouette, trying to keep his balance, but that old soccer injury makes him wobbly on one side, and his arms windmill, a frantic signal of some kind. He stares straight into my eyes as he falls backward, the look on his face saying, *This isn't at all what I had in mind.*

He makes a smaller splash than I would've imagined; he knifes into the water like he's slick and greased up. His head disappears, then quickly resurfaces. He spits river water, but there's something I don't expect. He has a smile on his face.

People who don't know this slow-flowing river don't understand the current. The constant, invisible tug beneath the surface sometimes catches them off guard. Colston's smile wavers when he realizes he is being pulled downstream. He knows how to swim, but not well, which surprises me. People with money are usually good swimmers. He treads water, his head bobbing just above the surface, but he's not making any progress back to the dock. I toss him the loose end of the rope I coiled not fifteen minutes earlier. Colston plays tug of war with the current, and I check to see how the new cleat holds. I see it straining a little, but it's firm. I'm glad I put a little elbow grease behind those nuts when I tightened them.

Colston reaches up, and that's when I notice the screaming on the hill behind me. Mary-Frazier must have spotted her husband doing a whirling dervish off the dock. "Oh my god, Colston!" she shrieks. "Oh my god!" When I look toward the noise, I can tell, even from this distance, that Ruby has given up. She stands at the porch rail, her arms crossing her chest. If she had a white flag, she'd wave it. I count that as a point in her favor; Ruby knows when to quit.

I hoist Colston onto the dock, and he drips like a happy dog. His full smile has returned. He rolls his eyes when he looks at his expensive loafers. Up the hill his wife paces back and forth the length of the porch. She's stopped yelling at us, probably because her husband is out of the water and clear of any advancing snake invasions. He waves at her. "Not to worry, sweets!" Then he turns to me. "The water is colder than I expected," he says. "That was really refreshing."

"A dunk in the river is always a good thing," I say.

He pulls his shirttail out and wrings water onto his loafers. "I'm going to make you an insane offer for this property," he says. "But you already know this, right? I'm going to offer you more than it's worth, thousands more, and the thing is, you're going to turn it down. You're not even going to consider it, are you? You were never going to sell."

I suddenly like Colston more than I thought I would. He doesn't bitch about falling in the river. He gets straight to the point. He predicts the future with an uncanny accuracy.

"Yeah, you pretty much called that one," I say. "I'm not selling. I don't know what I'm going to do, but I'm not selling. I'm waiting for something to strike me."

"You realize, you might never get struck. There are so many poor bastards who wait all their lives for a sign, and they never get the memo."

"Maybe I've already gotten a sign," I say, giving Colston a long look.

"Touché," he says. "This probably isn't a place for us anyway. Good to know."

We head back up the hill, Colston's loafers emitting a watery squeak with every step. "Do you have any sons?" I say, and the question stops him. I see him weighing the answers. It's a simple question, but he thinks this is a test, and if he aces it, I might change my mind about selling.

"No, no children," he says. "Mary-Frazier and I have not started a family. I haven't received a sign yet." Colston smiles.

He decides to go with the truth, another reason to like him, even if he might be making fun of me. I could tell the minute I laid eyes on them, he and ol' MF are too busy with themselves to ever worry about children.

"I have a son," I say. "Thom's thirteen. He fell in the river too. He says he cheated death. He might be a little dramatic."

This is the first time I've talked to a complete stranger about Thom. Most of the people I come across don't even know I have a son, and here I am, telling a dripping, smiling man in soggy loafers that there is this person in the world named Thom, and I am his father. I don't know what the feeling is, blooming in my chest, but it's weighty and warm, and it could bring tears to my eyes if I allowed it.

"He likes the river, I take it?" Colston says.

"He'll learn to," and that's the last thing we say on the walk back to the porch, like the two of us know there is nothing more to talk about.

40

Ruby isn't too upset with me for not selling. I'm not too upset with her for ambushing me with a pair of coastal carpetbaggers. As if she predicted somebody would take a dunk in the river, she has a clean towel in her Bronco. Colston spreads it across the driver's seat of his fancy SUV, and he and Mary-Frazier wave goodbye.

Ruby sits on the porch and slips off her shoes. "I had to try, you know," she said. "It's very weird for me. Half the time I deal with dead people; the other half, I negotiate with the living. I'm a lot more attracted to the dead ones. They are never disappointed. Did you see the look on Mary What's Her Name's face? Pure disappointment. You only get that from the living. Not too hard to make the dead happy."

"I hope they find something," I say, waving in the general direction of the highway. Willie Nelson scratches at the screen door, so I let him out, and he makes a beeline for Ruby's shins.

"Oh, they'll find something," she says, reaching to scratch Willie Nelson's ears. "They always do. The rich are hunter-gatherers, the modern kind. They go out and hunt and hunt and gather up houses. I'll keep my eye open for them." Ruby seems to be making herself comfortable. Down on the dock, the Old Man's hip joint glints in the sunshine. Ruby rubs her toes. "You're never leaving here, are you?" she says.

"I don't know," I say. "I don't like to get too far ahead of myself. Planning is not one of my strong suits. I got a job I don't like that I need to get back to. I have a house, but I just rent it. I guess neither one of those things is truly anchoring me."

"That's another reason I'm not real fond of men," she says. "Y'all spend most of your time looking for reasons not to do things. If you didn't have somebody kicking your ass some of the time, y'all would just stay inside and watch TV and eat the sandwiches somebody brings you." I didn't realize Ruby wasn't fond of men. I just thought it was me. That's the worst kind of ego you can have, thinking someone's dislike of you is your fault and not a general thing.

"My father just died, Ruby," I say.

"Your dead relative card is about to expire, sparky," she says, slipping her shoes back on and grimacing when she does it. "Stop whipping it out."

I hear the drone of Ruby's Bronco long after it's out of sight, and soon it's just me on the porch, the only sound the tiny whine of mosquitoes orbiting my ears. The sun is as high as it's going to get, and you wouldn't think the bugs would be out in the heat of the day. I might be sitting in the same chair where my father died. I wonder if the same mosquitoes that feasted on him are having a go at me right now? How long do mosquitoes live? They may have one of those twenty-four-hour life spans, one of those breed-and-die existences. I'll bet the Old Man sensed that. He didn't die because he was too tired or too sick. He just knew it was time to shut it down, him and the mosquitoes.

I'm not a smart man. There are times I don't do the right things when the right things ought to be done. I should probably sell this property. I could pocket more money than I've ever seen in my life. I could replace the pickup. I could take the edge off that dull, anxious ache I get at the end of every month, when I play a shell game between the bills coming in and money going out. But I'm not selling. I belong here, and I think the Old Man knew that. He realized if he could get me back here long enough to watch the river run, I'd stay. Another thing about rivers, I guess. They always carry something with them, most of it we can see—the fallen cypress needles, the bubbly foam in the eddies, driftwood, angry snakes. But the current also carries things we never see all that clearly, can only feel in our blood and bones. In its slow, steady movement, this river carries memory and nostalgia and stories we've forgotten and stories we never want to retell. Maybe it even carries the ends of stories, the last acts. Maybe if I stare at the water and squint my eyes in the sun, I can see that afternoon when the Old Man brought me to the black water and let me wash the scent of Lonnie Tisdale's funeral off my skin. Maybe I can see my mother, wondering where her husband is, imagining the worst, when the worst isn't all that bad—just a man sitting alone, watching the river drift past his sliver of sand.

Just like I'm doing right now. That's why I can't sell this place, because this place was always waiting for me. I had to figure that out. Like I said, I'm not a smart man.

"Dammit, Ruby, you don't give up, do you?" I say to no one, except maybe Willie Nelson and the mosquitoes. She's doubled back on me. I hear the engine lumbering down the sand road, a couple tenths of a mile away. But when the sound pulls into sight, it's not Ruby, but the Mercury Cougar. Linda always seems to know where I am.

The way the bright sun splashes off her windshield, I don't catch sight of Linda until she kills the engine and climbs out. She waves up to the porch, but stands beside the car, as if she's waiting on something. She knows she doesn't need an invitation. She has the strangest grin on her face.

Then I see what's keeping her close to the car. A couple more doors open. Roma and Thom climb out.

"We have surprised you, Elwin!" Thom calls up to me. He holds a large pizza box in front of him like a tray. I stand too quickly from my seat, and my head goes a little light, and for a split second, I don't trust what I see. But it's not a mirage in the heat. "We brought pepperoni!"

I'm still trying to figure it all out when the three of them mount the porch. Roma carries napkins and paper plates. Linda must have reached back into the Mercury and grabbed a small cooler. They are smiling. Even Willie Nelson is excited. He can't decide which pair of legs to wind around.

"You want this all explained, don't you," Roma says. "Okay, we were headed out of town, and I thought, 'You know, I haven't said goodbye to Linda,' so I figured we could find that old house you grew up in. Thom knew she lived near it. He says you've told that story so many times."

"#4, Elwin," Thom says.

"It took us a while," Roma says.

"But they showed up at my door," Linda says.

"We spotted the Cougar in her driveway," Roma says. "It wasn't hard. It stands out. I mean that in a good way, Linda. No offense."

"Oh, none taken. What does everyone want to drink?"

Linda places sodas on the small table, then turns to me. "I had a couple of these left in the fridge. I'll never drink them," she says. She pulls two Old Milwaukees from the cooler. The Old Man's brand. The sight of the Old Milwaukee sticks a pebble in my throat.

"I'll take one," Roma says, and pops the top. I like that about Roma. The way she barrels into things, she always takes the painful sharpness off hard moments. It's a talent she doesn't know she possesses. She has no idea how much it means to see those cans of beer.

"I still don't get it," I say.

"Of course you don't," Roma says.

"But you were going home," I say. "We told each other goodbye. I was coming down here to close things up. You just missed Ruby. She brought a couple who wanted to buy the house. The guy fell in the river."

"Did he cheat death?" Thom asks.

"Barely," I say.

Roma looks around, scanning for evidence. "Did you close things up? Did you accept an offer? Doesn't look like anything's changed to me."

"Well, no."

"Exactly," Roma says. "You know, Elwin, sometimes you

think about situations too much. Here's the deal. We went to Linda's house, and we decided we weren't ready to leave yet. We decided that you might be going through something rough and emotional that we could help with. We decided that bringing you a pepperoni pizza and an Old Milwaukee was more important than us getting home before dark."

"We wanted to help you say goodbye to this place," Linda says. "Or say hello."

"Yes, Elwin, don't overthink," Thom says around a mouthful of pizza. "It's not healthy. Trust me, I know."

I sit in the chair and reach for the other beer. The sun has shifted behind the shack now, and we're grateful for the shade easing across the porch. They are right. Sometimes I try too hard to slide all the pieces of the puzzle together, especially when it's better to let them lie jumbled. I haven't had this feeling since I was a kid, the one that warms you up, even when you're in the shade. There is a family sitting in front of me, and it's mine.

Don't think any further than that, Elwin.

41

Through the shank of the afternoon, we sit and eat and talk and make plans and bat at mosquitoes. We don't know how any of this is going to work, but that doesn't stop us from putting words into the air. Everyone pulls their chairs closer, into a tight little circle. Nobody thinks it's a bad idea for me to move to the river. In fact, they are so enthusiastic about it, I feel like they are trying to get rid of me.

"One way to think about it," Roma says, "is that Thom will have a vacation every time y'all get together down here. And you can still do your weekends at my house, only with a little extra driving. You can sleep on the pull-out. It's not that far away." Roma has never asked me to stay at her house. It's funny—the idea of me being farther away seems to be cutting down the distances between the three of us.

"And there's Lily, of course," Thom says, the shiny confidence in his voice suggesting he and Lily will be together forever, forever sneaking around the breezeway near the soda machine and exchanging awkward kisses. I want to tell him things like that—thirteen-year-old things—rarely last, but there's no need to burst his romantic bubble. At least I have learned that much about parenting; you can't possibly fill up all the potholes in your kid's road. They have to hit them on their own. Lily Salters will probably break Thom's heart again, but this time, when it happens at The All Excellent Inn, we'll have a dock to sit on and talk about it.

"Sure," I say. "You and Lily can visit all you want when you come see me." Roma's head tilts toward me at an odd angle, like she's waiting for something to happen. Then it occurs to me: she offered up her sofa, but I never mentioned anything about her accommodations if she brings Thom down. "We'll figure out something for your mom, some place for her to stay."

"You ought to close in underneath the house. You could put a bedroom and a bath down there. My cousin is a contractor too. You know, the one who put the holes in Hubert's hip joint?" Linda says. I'm beginning to wonder if everybody in this county has more than one vocation. A contractor/drill press operator. A real estate agent/funeral home director.

"Hubert?" Roma says. "What the hell? That's your father's name? I've never heard you call him anything but the Old Man."

"Yeah, Hubert," I say. "He really hated that name."

"He didn't hate it that much," Linda says, quietly, like she's embarrassed to reveal that she knows more about my father than I do. "He just thought it didn't fit him."

I remember the ceramic chicken squatting on the floorboard of my truck. "Hold on," I say and quick-walk out to the pickup to grab it. When I return and place it in her lap, I say, "Did you know that the Old Man—I mean, Hubert—left this for you in his will? I kept forgetting to give it to you. I'm sorry. There was a lot going on."

"Oh my," Linda says. "That chicken." She cradles the bird as if it might come alive.

"It's filled up with—" I catch myself. If it's a surprise, I don't want to spoil it.

"Oh my," she repeats. "You know, I always saw that chicken up on his fridge, but I never thought much about it. I always thought it was something left over from his old house. Maybe something your mother had. I thought it must have some sentimental value. None of my business, you know."

I want to tell her that the chicken is, indeed, chock full of sentimental value, but again, not my place. I don't need to spoil anything for her or give her any kind of preview. Thom breaks up the awkward space in the conversation.

"Well, open it, Linda," he says. "It's your chicken now."

Linda sets the chicken on the small table to her right. "I don't know," she says. "Should I?"

"Of course," Roma says. "This is the perfect place to do it."

"It could be empty," Thom says, proving that his ability to

cut to the chase is not always helpful. Linda could be worried that the ceramic chicken may be all there is. She gently removes the head of the bird and tilts the body toward her a little to use some of the late afternoon light that filters through the cypress and pines.

"Oh my," she whispers. She knows what fills up the chicken without reaching in, but she pulls out a small handful of ticket stubs anyway and lets them rain between her fingers. "I had no idea. Why, I think he kept every single one." Thom reaches over and grabs a stub that fell to the tabletop, reading it in the light.

Linda's voice begins to wilt, and tears well in her eyes. She reaches in again and feels the roll of cash. She pulls it into the light. "Oh my," she says again, keeping the money at arm's length, like it might be venomous. She wipes her eyes with her free hand and sees the note, takes it in. That's when she begins to cry for real.

"Who am I going to see movies with now?" Linda says between quick breaths. "He kept every single one. What am I going to do now?" She blinks and tears roll down her cheeks.

Roma reaches over and puts her arm around Linda's shoulders. "That's so sweet, Linda. You meant so much to him, I can tell." Linda leans in a little against Roma.

"I've got it! Elwin can take you to the movies!" Thom says. He sounds like a scientist who's discovered a new element. "You can still go to movies." I don't want to tell him that it's not about going to the movies and getting ticket stubs and eating popcorn. I could take Linda to a hundred movies, and it would never be the same. He doesn't understand that it's all about who sits next to you. He's got so much to learn. I've got so much to teach him.

"Of course I can take you, Linda," I say. "I'd be honored."

Linda hugs the headless chicken to her chest and stares down into the ticket stubs. "Oh my," she says one last time, then she smiles. "We had such good times."

And just like that, the rest of us have tears in our eyes, even Thom. Maybe he's learning more than I realize.

42

It's too late in the evening for Roma and Thom to drive all the way home. I don't want them on the road after dark. I remind her that I still have room 113 at The All Excellent Inn, so she and Thom can stay there one more night. Marvin will like having somebody in one of his rooms. I can spend the night at the shack.

"Plus, you can see Lily one more time," I say.

"Actually, Elwin, I think I'd like to stay out here with you. Lily and I said our goodbyes for now. Another one would appear redundant," Thom says. "May I spend the night here?" I resist the urge to glance at the single bed. I don't want Thom to think he isn't welcome. I'll figure it out. Sleep in a deck chair if I have to.

Roma appears a little hurt, but I think she gets it. My son wants to spend the night with me. And she can extend her Independence Celebration yet another few hours. Maybe she and Marvin will roll up a big, fat one, wrangle a couple of lawn chairs poolside and watch the evening melt into complete darkness.

Linda has a tight grip on her ceramic chicken. Perhaps I never conceded that the Old Man could love someone other than my mother. Or rather, have a different *kind* of love than the one he had for her. I'm not even sure that was love. The Old Man and my mother occupied their separate little worlds that spun around each other. She had her nursing—working shifts at the old hospital or driving into the county for home health visits. She used to take Eli and me with her on those calls. I haven't thought about Eli in days. But that's exactly what Eli wanted, to be so separated that he becomes forgotten. My mother had her nursing and her two boys. The Old Man had his little spit of land on Black River and his Old Milwaukees and the Vietnam legacies that ate at his stomach and his brain. How do you ever know when you have enough?

"I can take you back to the motel," Linda says. She's not crying anymore, but there's a ragged husk on her voice.

Roma thanks her and says, "And you're good with the cat here?"

On cue, Willie Nelson appears on the porch steps and stares at us like we're criminals. Willie Nelson is the first nomad cat I've ever met. Thom is correct: Willie Nelson could live anywhere he lands. Now he's landed at the shack, back on the riverbank. He looks comfortable, sitting splay-legged on the top step, licking his back thigh.

"He'll be okay," I say. "I don't know much about cats, but I probably don't need to know a lot when it comes to Willie Nelson. He'll take care of me more than me of him." Willie Nelson finishes his licking and sprints down the steps as if he's left a stove burning somewhere.

"I'm fine with the entire arrangement," Thom says and waves his arms like a benediction. Five minutes later Linda and Roma disappear into the last of the late afternoon, the brake lights a couple of red eyes winking through the trees, and it's just me and Thom in the sandy, two-rut driveway.

"Elwin, I think we should go to the dock before it gets completely dark," Thom says, and without waiting for an answer, he starts down the slope to the river. Willie Nelson appears from under the shack and takes up the pace behind Thom's heels.

I've had enough time on the dock today, what with screwing in the Old Man's hip joint and pulling Colston out of the river, but I don't want Thom down there by himself. I'm responsible for him tonight, and he still isn't completely comfortable around the water. That's going to take a while.

Thom already has his shoes off, his legs dangling in the black current. There's plenty of soft, late-afternoon light, so I scan the river's surface, checking for the wriggle of a snake making its way toward the dock. When something vibrates the surface of the water—like a pair of dangling legs—a cottonmouth might mistake it for an animal in distress, trying to swim to safety. In other words, supper. But Black River is smooth as a pool table. I barely detect a current moving toward the coast.

Thom doesn't look over when I sit beside him. "Things are changing fast," he says. "You've seen those old movies, haven't you, Elwin? Those silent films, where all the people operate in fast motion? That's what I feel like right now—like everything is approaching me in fast motion." He swishes his legs in the current, and Willie Nelson peers over the edge of the dock, waiting for something magical in the ripples. I've never seen a cat so comfortable around water. Maybe that's what happens when you grow up feral on a riverbank. "It feels like we've been here for a month, so much has happened."

"That's the way the world spins when you're thirteen," I say. "You don't have time to breathe. You'll have time for that later."

"Do you think Lily will forget me?" my son asks.

I want to tell him that, yes, of course she'll forget you. But she'll tuck you away somewhere in the back of her mind, and you'll appear now and again, like a ghost. She'll remember the way the breezeway felt under her feet when you leaned in to kiss her. She'll remember the taste of your mouth. She'll remember the way the rain smelled. She'll remember, but only when your ghost makes an appearance.

"You're going to visit her when you come see me, right? That way, she can't forget you," I say, which seems like a safer, less painful answer.

"Yes, but that can't go on forever, Elwin," Thom says, tossing a bit of condescension in my direction. "That's not possible." Thom is already getting over Lily. His first crush is fading, and he isn't sure he wants it to. More thirteen-year-old shit I can't explain to him.

"You and Lily will be fine," I say. "It always works out." Which is a lie. Sometimes it doesn't work out. Sometimes, it's just over, which I suppose is fine too. Everything is carried away, like life has its own deep-flowing current that you can't see. We're all on a river, whether we know it or not.

"Elwin, that looks suspiciously like Private's fake hip," Thom says, his voice rising. "Did you put that there? That is an odd place for a hip joint."

Only at that moment does it strike me that screwing your dead father's old titanium hip joint to a rotting dock might seem psychotic. Or desperate. I don't know why I did it. I didn't think much about it.

"That's extremely cool," Thom says, running his hand over the ball end of the prosthetic. "It's still warm from the sun. It must absorb the heat."

I'm sure he's about to explain the heat conducting properties of titanium, but instead, Thom stands and peels off his shirt. "I'm getting in the water," he says, and a thousand bad thoughts fly into my head. I scan the river again for the signatures of snakes on the surface. He doesn't know how strong the current can be just a couple of feet down. Colston felt it a few hours ago. It's not an undertow, but it's sneaky strong. It's all on me now, here on this dock that I own, on this patch of land that was bequeathed to me a few days ago. I don't know how deep my own water is. There could be something lurking there that we can't see, can only feel. Lonnie Tisdale must have known that. I glance quickly into the water for Lonnie Tisdale's face to appear, but he's gone for good. We've finally said our goodbyes. I'm sure of that.

I point at the water with my foreshortened finger, the wrapping dull in the last light of the afternoon. "I'm not sure," I say, and Thom looks where I'm pointing, like I'm warning him about something.

"Not sure about what?" he says. "I'm going to leave on my underwear. I don't want to get my shorts wet. Is that okay?" Without waiting for my answer, he unbuckles his pants and drops them to the dock. He's wearing bright Star Wars boxers. I laugh without thinking.

"Excuse me, Elwin," Thom says, "but I like Star Wars. I'm not committing a crime." I would have guessed he'd be embarrassed, but he sounds proud of his loyalty to the franchise.

"And they are really comfortable." He hitches up the waistband and dips a toe off the dock into the water.

I give the river another quick scan. The sun is about to drop below the tree line, and the last of the day sifts through the cypress branches and pine needles. There's still plenty of light, but it's going to fade fast. I'm sure there's a three-quarter moon tonight, but I don't know *why* I know. The mosquitoes haven't found us yet, but they'll show up soon. I'm sure of that too.

"Does it feel weird, Elwin," he says, "deciding to live where your father died?" He sits on the edge of the dock again and dangles his legs. He's easing himself into the water a few inches at a time.

"I guess I don't view it that way," I say, which is the truth. I don't feel like I'm subbing in for the Old Man. I don't consider myself taking over the reins or anything. "I mean, sometimes you don't realize what you're supposed to do with yourself, until it sort of slaps you in the face. I didn't plan on any of this."

"Like Lily," Thom says. "I certainly didn't plan on meeting her."

"That's the best part," I say. "If we only get what we're expecting, life becomes boring, you know?" Thom slides more of his legs below the surface. They are so white against the black water. "How was that kiss?" I ask, without considering how the question might come off when it hits his ears.

"Oh, so you know about that?" Thom says. "Elwin, there are certain events I should keep to myself. I'm sure you'll understand." He considers flopping into the water, then stops. "I think Mother is happy you're moving here. I don't mean to say that she's glad you won't be in town. She's happy that you're happy. You do seem happier, Elwin. And if you think about it, you should be sad because your father is recently deceased. But you're happy. Interesting."

Thom is right. What I've been feeling the last couple of days is happiness. Some part of me knew I was going to move here before the thought arrived fully formed in my brain. Maybe it was part of a plan. The Old Man's plan.

Thom drops into the river, and his head disappears for a couple of seconds, which makes me suck in a quick breath. When he surfaces, he spews water and begins treading. My son really does know how to swim. "Elwin, this feels wonderful," he says. "It's so chilly a few feet down, where you can't see."

I could tell him that most of Black River flows where you can't see it. So many things camouflaged in the darkness, lurking where it's chillier. Things you find when you least expect it. Lonnie Tisdale found them, a couple of times, actually. Once he lost an eye. The second time he didn't break the surface again until the sheriff's deputy reeled him in. My father brought me to the river because he knew one thing: even though a river can kill, it also has the power to heal. Something about water, I suppose.

"Maybe Roma would let me spend my summers here, more than just a couple of weeks," Thom says, already making plans for his future. I love that my son is looking forward to things. I could learn from him.

Thom drifts a few feet away from the dock, then breaststrokes back. He's not a great swimmer, but he's strong enough to handle the tug of the river. "Don't worry, Elwin," he says. "I'm not attempting to cheat death or anything silly like that."

Thom reaches up and grabs the Old Man's hip joint that's been converted into a cleat. He lets his legs flow behind him in the current, while he holds on to the ball. That's when he notices his wrist. "Oh no, help me, Elwin," he says. "I forgot to take off the watch."

I reach down and unstrap it from his wrist. "Have I ruined it?" he says. "Is it still waterproof?"

The second hand isn't moving, but maybe he's just forgotten to wind it. I don't see any water under the crystal. "It's fine," I say. No need to make Thom feel bad about swimming in the river. The watch has served its purpose. I put it in my pocket. "Nothing to worry about."

Thom swaps hands on the new cleat. "Look at this, Elwin," he says. "Private is keeping me safe. He gives me something to hold on to." Thom grins like a Christmas-morning kid.

I undo the button on my jeans and let them fall. I'm not wearing Star Wars boxers. I've got on saggy briefs, like always. Like Thom, my legs blaze white in the fading light. Thom laughs at the sight of me without pants, which I probably deserve. I dive flatly into the water, making sure I don't slice too deep. I don't know what's down there yet.

When I break the dark surface, I keep my eyes squeezed shut, and my ears fill with river water, softening any of the sounds around me, but I hear my son somewhere on my right, probably still clinging to a piece of the Old Man.

"Don't get out of sight, Elwin," he yells at me, but he's not scared. He sounds safe, if safe could make a noise. "Stay where I can see you."

Those words are ghostly and familiar, bouncing back to me like an echo that has been aging for years and years. Thom doesn't have to worry. This river isn't dragging me away. I'll be here.